Arrangements

by Ken Weitzman

A SAMUEL FRENCH ACTING EDITION

SAMUEL FRENCH

FOUNDED 1830

NEW YORK HOLLYWOOD LONDON TORONTO

SAMUELFRENCH.COM

MUSIC USE NOTE

Licensees are solely responsible for obtaining formal written permission from copyright owners to use copyrighted music in the performance of this play and are strongly cautioned to do so. If no such permission is obtained by the licensee, then the licensee must use only original music that the licensee owns and controls. Licensees are solely responsible and liable for all music clearances and shall indemnify the copyright owners of the play and their licensing agent, Samuel French, Inc., against any costs, expenses, losses and liabilities arising from the use of music by licensees.

IMPORTANT BILLING AND CREDIT REQUIREMENTS

All producers of *ARRANGEMENTS must* give credit to the Author of the Play in all programs distributed in connection with performances of the Play, and in all instances in which the title of the Play appears for the purposes of advertising, publicizing or otherwise exploiting the Play and/or a production. The name of the Author *must* appear on a separate line on which no other name appears, immediately following the title and *must* appear in size of type not less than fifty percent of the size of the title type.

ARRANGEMENTS was originally produced in the UCSD Baldwin New Play Festival in April, 2002. It was directed by Suzanne Agins, with set design by Ryan Palmer, lighting design by Jason Thompson, and costume design by Raquel Barreto. The production stage manager was Collin Larkins. The cast was as follows:

DONNA .... Makela Spielman

ROBBY. .... Adam Smith

ROS. ....Christine Albright

KEITH.. ....Corey Brill

DAVID ....Michael Keyloun

HOMELESS MAN (and offstage characters).................. Ismet Prcic

ARRANGEMENTS was subsequently produced by the Atlantic Theatre Company (managing director, Andrew D. Hamingson; Neil Pepe, artistic director) in January 2005. It was directed by Christian Parker, with set design by Nathan Heverin, lighting design by Josh Bradford, costume design by Theresa Squire, and original music and sound by Matthew Puckett. The production stage manager was Freda Farrell. The cast was as follows:

DONNA ....Katy Grenfell

ROBBY. .... Ben Walker

ROS. ....Julia Murney

KEITH.. ....Chris Duva

DAVID ....Stephen Kunken

HOMELESS MAN (and offstage characters).............. Michael Warner

ARRANGEMENTS received developmental support from the Mark Taper Forum, Atlantic Theatre Company, Cherry Lane Alternative, Arena Stage, Florida Stage, and the Williamstown Theatre Festival.

ARRANGEMENTS received the 2003 L. Arnold Weissberger Award

CHARACTERS

(In order of appearance)

ROBBY – 19, passionate, exuberant, impressionable. Lost and searching.

DAVID – Robbie's older brother. Late 20s to early 30s. Married. Desperate for his planning ways to rub off on Robby.

DONNA – Obese, late-30s. Sexy, smart, fierce and funny. Raging conflict between exploding Ros's life for her sister's own good and trying desperately to stay connected to her. Regardless of havoc she wreaks, she always believes it's the right thing to do.

ROS – Donna's younger sister. Mid-30s. Co-owner of the flower shop. Obsessively body-conscious for fear of becoming Donna. Fights desperately to remain in control.

KEITH – Ros's business partner and 'lover' in that order. Late-30s. Terrified of chaos. Phobic. Capable of sudden explosive outbursts.

HOMELESS MAN – Imposing.

FITNESS INSTRUCTOR (played by the same actor playing the Homeless Man) – Offstage voice. A peppy guru.

O.A. SPEAKER (played by the same actor playing the Homeless Man) – Offstage voice. Sincere.

SETTING

Multiple locations: best if spare or representational. The above world/ below world layout of the flower shop is important but can be expressed by a matter of inches. Scenes should flow easily and quickly into one another.

TIME

The present.

AUTHOR'S NOTE

It is important to keep in mind that the characters in this play are desperately trying to save one another, though they may go about oing so in circuitous, troubling, or destructive ways.

Stakes should be very high, outsized, even for seemingly small things; a heightened reality. Nothing is casual. This is not a small, intimate, psychological play. Emotions are real but all is anxious, urgent; not false, but heightened.

ACKNOWLEDGEMENTS

The author wishes to thank...

Adele Shank and Allan Havis, Ken and Ginger Baldwin, Christian Parker, Suzie Agins, Les Waters, the Anna L. Weissberger Foundation, Amy Levinson, Wendy Goldberg, Michael Ritchie, Chris Till, Mead Hunter, Pier Carlo Talenti.

A special thank you to Makela Spielman who originated the role of Donna, and whose artistry and ideas are forever stiched into the fabric of the character; and to Amy Cook, my wife and dramaturg, for so, so much.

—Ken Weitzman

PROLOGUE

(Spotlight on **ROBBY**. *He displays a McDonald's ham-burger. Perhaps music accompanies his slam, perhaps a few applause or shouts along the way. Energy.)*

ROBBY. Do you know what's been found in here?

Do you know?

Everything.

Everything in the world.

You name it.

Hair, finger nails, skin, sweat, rat feces, human feces.

Keys, coins, jewelry, a bullet,

suntan lotion, toilet tissue.

It's all in there.

It's no wonder

then.

No wonder at all,

they didn't hesitate

when we came in.

Bring it to the back,

they said.

Bring it to the back.

They didn't even care...

to hear her note.

(Lights down on **ROBBY**, *up on* **DONNA**, *morbidly obese and in her late thirties to early forties. She sits in a chair in her robe and slippers. She is motionless, staring out before her. Blackout.)*

Scene One

*(**DAVID**'s apartment, night. **DAVID**, in his early 30s, cuts out an article from the paper as **ROBBY**, 19, fidgets continuously, a caged animal.)*

DAVID. The window was smashed. They broke right in.

*(expecting **ROBBY** to respond)*

Our downstairs neighbors. Their car. Broken into.

ROBBY. I heard you.

DAVID. Parked on this block when it happened. Fifteen feet from here. Of course they didn't take the proper precautions. Robby.

ROBBY. Fifteen feet. What?

DAVID. *(meaningfully)* Their glove compartment was closed.

ROBBY. So?

DAVID. So!? So you have to leave it open. Show them there isn't anything in it. Leave it open and empty. That's one. *Two*: no loose change. Anywhere. *Three*: The club. Visual deterrent.

ROBBY. If someone really wants to break in –

DAVID. *Four*: I go back and forth on four. To lock the doors or not.

ROBBY. What? My brother leave his car door unlocked?

DAVID. Instead of having your window smashed or your lock destroyed you let them in easy, so they can check, find nothing, leave. That's not the issue.

ROBBY. What's the issue?

DAVID. The homeless. Your car unlocked, you wake up the next morning and find a guy sleeping in your back seat.

*(**ROBBY** gets up and exits offstage to **DAVID**'s kitchen. **DAVID** resumes with the article, highlighting parts of it.)*

DAVID. You better listen to what I'm telling you, Robby.

ROBBY. *(from offstage)* I don't even own a car!

DAVID. You have to learn how to live in the city now.

(*No answer from* **ROBBY**.)

What are you looking for?

ROBBY. (*entering with a box of cereal*) Something to eat before I go.

DAVID. Whatever you want.

(*looking up*)

Not that.

ROBBY. It's full.

DAVID. (*holding the one he's cut out*) A new article in the paper today. About partially hydrogenated oils. Trans fats. Even worse than we thought. They're deadly. A trans fat is a fatty oil transmogrified into a semi-solid. You know what that does? It causes impaired cellular function, clogged arteries and degenerative disease. I'm taking that cereal back to the supermarket tomorrow. Show them the article. Imagine, they're still selling this, in this day and age, with all the information out there. I'm just glad Jill didn't eat any. Direct pipeline of poison right to the baby.

ROBBY. Is Jill pregnant?

DAVID. No.

But we might start trying.

ROBBY. You might?

DAVID. I still...I cannot believe you got expelled...I cannot grasp that.

(**ROBBY** *puts on his jacket to go.*)

DAVID. Dad should have taken you in.

ROBBY. Yeah, well...it was a bit of a shock when I showed up.

DAVID. So he bars you from the house? Stops talking to you?

(**ROBBY** *says nothing.*)

Why aren't you angry at him?

ROBBY. He…he's got a lot going on.

DAVID. What does that mean? Like what? What does he have going on?

(suddenly panicked)

Robby?

ROBBY. *(covering)* I don't know. Like…I don't know. Retirement. Just retirement I guess.

DAVID. It's too early for him to retire.

ROBBY. David –

DAVID. It is too early!

(ROBBY checks his watch.)

ROBBY. I should go.

(He grabs the cereal and starts to exit.)

DAVID. Put that down.

ROBBY. It's breakfast for a week.

DAVID. I won't let you put that inside you.

ROBBY. It's just cereal.

DAVID. "It's just cereal, it's just college, it's just my life!" You travel on a slippery slope. I'm terrified for you Robby, of where you're headed. Terrified. Aren't you?

ROBBY. I don't know. Maybe.

DAVID. Sit down Robby. Sit.

(ROBBY sits.)

DAVID. The money I gave you –

ROBBY. I appreciate it, I really –

DAVID. It has strings attached.

(He pulls out a piece of paper and hands it to ROBBY, who looks at it, confused.)

DAVID. It's a contract. In exchange for my paying your security deposit and first month's rent – you will meet with me three times a week.

ROBBY. David, I'll pay you back.

DAVID. *(holds out a pen)* Three times a week and you won't have to.

*(when **ROBBY** hesitates)*

If you don't sign, I'll ask your landlord for the security back. You'll have to move in with me and Jill.

*(Faced with that alternative, **ROBBY** quickly takes the pen, signs. **DAVID** takes the contract. He gives **ROBBY** the highlighted, cut-out article.)*

DAVID. Read this for next time. I'm going to quiz you on it.

*(**ROBBY** takes it unhappily.)*

DAVID. It's not like you have other homework to do.

*(**ROBBY** starts off.)*

DAVID. And call me the second you walk in your door. Don't forget this time.

*(Lights go down on **DAVID**'s apartment as **ROBBY** bolts into a spotlight.)*

ROBBY. Excuse me ma'am. Excuse me.

Put that down.

I said put that cereal down right now.

You don't want to buy that.

You don't want to eat that.

Put it back on the shelf

It's for your own health.

Didn't you read the side panel?

It has partially hydrogenated soybean oil.

I said partially hydrogenated soybean oil.

It's faster than the plague

It's quicker than cancer

It don't give a shit you got the body of a dancer.

(Scattered applause from a small audience.)

It's instant heart attack

You're dead on the spot

It works even faster than if you got shot.

ROBBY. *(cont.)* Your arteries clogged
    With the *trans* fat
    Your arteries explode just like that.
    So put that back on the shelf
    And start to scan
    Cheerios, Frosted Flakes, Raisin Bran.
    "Examine every panel
    It's not that big a feat"
    And by the time you're fucking finished, there's
    nothing left
    to eat!

(Applause. Lights down on **ROBBY**. *Up on* **DONNA**, *again sitting in a chair, but now dressed. A suitcase and an oversized handbag sit next to the chair.* **DONNA** *stares out in front of her, in a trance. Blackout.)*

Scene Two

(The backroom office of the Ros-Farmer Flower Shop. The office is very neatly arranged, containing antiques, rustic accoutrements, vases, and other tasteful touches. There is a desk/work table and a futon-couchbed with Donna's suitcase beside it. There are three exits. One leads to the bathroom, one to the front of the store and the other down below to the basement [which will be seen]. The door and the stairs that lead down to the basement may or may not be seen. If seen, the door should be sturdy. A finished flower arrangement sits on the worktable. Next to it a neatly folded pile of clothes.)

*(***ROS***, mid 30s, stands on top of a crate. She is in her bra and underwear only. She is very still. Her arms are lifted out from her body slightly for better viewing of them. Several feet behind her stands* **KEITH**, *early 40s, and co-owner of the flower shop. He is perfectly still, studying* **ROS**. *He holds a magic marker in his hand.)*

(A world of tension between them. Pause.)

ROS. It's fab. Is it not fab?

KEITH. What?

ROS. The arrangement. It's fabege.

(KEITH *says nothing. Still behind her, he steps over for a slightly different angle to study her.*)

ROS. It's fabulicious.

(*nothing from* KEITH)

Gwyneth Pierpont's breath will be swept from her body.

(KEITH *pops the cap off the marker, steps towards* ROS, *but not too close. Never too close.* ROS *tenses her arms.*)

KEITH. No flexing.

ROS. I've been working very hard on my triceps.

(KEITH *considers, then lowers the marker. He bends down and studies the back of* ROS' *legs.*)

ROS. That time of the month.

(KEITH *recoils.*)

ROS. No, sorry, I mean for us. For this.

(KEITH *returns, briefly looks at her from behind, then moves around to* ROS' *front side, again several feet away from her.* ROS *smiles tentatively, relieved for now. She maintains her position, looking up and over* KEITH.)

ROS. Been almost a year. Since the first time. Our first business meeting.

(*when* KEITH *does not respond*)

Me, the talented freelance designer. You, with the spreadsheets, the business plan.

(*a beat*)

Remember?

(KEITH *moves in [maintaining an arm's length distance] and circles* ROS' *stomach, then her hips, then her thighs.*)

KEITH. All the places you will be fat. You have the fat gene.

ROS. No.

(**KEITH** *moves back to the work table.* **ROS** *remains atop the crate, in shock.*)

KEITH. She does and she's your sister. Did you...is that how you used to look?

ROS. I've told you. I had the slightest of weight issues a loooong time ago.

KEITH. You were born of the same place.

(**ROS** *steps down and walks toward the worktable where* **KEITH** *is. He scurries to the other side of the table, thinking* **ROS** *is coming on to him.*)

KEITH. Stop. Stop. We talked about this. We talked about this!

(**ROS** *gets to the table and picks her shirt off the pile of folded clothes. She starts to put it on.*)

KEITH. Oh. I thought...I have rules.

ROS. I know you do. That's how I knew we'd be good together.

(**KEITH** *draws a circle on his forehead.*)

KEITH. I'm a fathead.

ROS. Oh darling. No need for that.

(*She puts on her pants.*)

KEITH. I should know. You'd only get fat if you get pregnant.

(**ROS** *stops.*)

KEITH. If we get married, after the business takes off, pretty soon you're going to want a baby.

(**ROS** *says nothing.*)

You'll want one just like my first wife. And after that, forget it. You'll be all stretched out and flabby.

ROS. I don't want a baby.

KEITH. No?

ROS. No.

KEITH. YOU LET YOUR FAT FUCKING SISTER INTO OUR STORE!

ROS. I didn't let her in! She, she just showed up. I don't even know how she found me.

KEITH. With our first important event coming up. The one that could make our business. Just one of these type of women hire you, it goes well, soon her whole circle of socialites are calling.

ROS. It will go well.

KEITH. She's fickle, that Gwyneth Pierpont. Seven changes. Seven. Over eighty-six percent of the original order. What if she sees your sister?

(*Lights come up on* **DONNA**, *entering McDonald's. She sits, placing her tray down, as well as her large shoulder bag. the tray is filled with multiple burgers, large drinks, and fries. During the following, she eats and drinks. In the office,* **ROS** *and* **KEITH** *turn and awkwardly focus on the flower arrangement. Small pause.*)

KEITH. Everything needs to go exactly as planned.

ROS. It will.

(**DONNA** *belches loudly.* **ROS** *seems to hear it. Or sense it. A tight smile through clenched teeth. She looks at her watch.*)

ROS. I should…I won't be long.

(*She exits.*)

Scene Three

(*A city bus.* **ROBBY** *stands. A large* **MAN** *in dirty clothes stands opposite him, stares.* **ROBBY** *notices him and turns away. The* **MAN** *continues to stare.* **ROBBY** *meets his gaze.*)

ROBBY. What?

(*The* **MAN** *lifts his shirt, exposing his bare chest.*)

MAN. This is a map of Jesus.

(*points to just below his ribs*)

And this is where I feed him.

(A beat. The **MAN** *holds out his hand.* **ROBBY,** *taken aback, fishes into his pocket for a quarter, hands it to him.)*

Scene Four

*(***ROS** *and* **DONNA** *at a table at McDonald's.* **ROS** *watches* **DONNA** *eat. Her eating is continuous but is neither voracious nor manic; it's more matter-of-fact.)*

*(***DONNA** *slurps the last of one of her giant drinks. She smiles at* **ROS.** *It fades as* **ROS** *does not smile in return. Pause.)*

DONNA. *(offering it out)* Fry?

*(***ROS** *takes it and throws it at* **DONNA.***)*

ROS. Don't you play games with me. Why are you here?

DONNA. I wanted to see you. It's been a long time.

ROS. Why?

DONNA. You're so suspicious.

*(***ROS** *waits.)*

DONNA. I'd like to reconcile.

(a beat)

ROS. Well go ahead. Reconcile.

*(***DONNA** *eats, says nothing.)*

ROS. That was quite an apology. I'm overwhelmed.

DONNA. You want me to apologize?

ROS. It seems a reasonable request from someone whose tried to sabotage my life.

DONNA. That's not true.

ROS. My paintings? You sit there and tell me that wasn't sabotage?

DONNA. I was –

ROS. No. No. I will not listen to your delusional rationales.

*(***DONNA** *resumes eating.)*

DONNA. *(under her breath)* They're not delusional.

*(**ROS** gets up and starts to leave.)*

DONNA. *(factual)* Scott's dying.

*(**ROS** stops.)*

DONNA. I've been waiting for the phone call. To be noti-fied. That's all that's left.

(curious)

Now every time a phone rings, the sound runs right through me. Echoes inside me, like I'm hollow. The sound bouncing around and around. It doesn't stop.

ROS. Where is he?

DONNA. With his lover.

*(**ROS** hesitates then sits back down. Pause.)*

ROS. What about, what about a job? Don't you have a job down there?

DONNA. Jenny Craig Fitness. I was fired.

*(from **ROS**' reaction)*

Not for my weight. It's actually part of their corporate strategy to have someone like me in the sales depart-ment. It's in the manual. A customer comes in, sits with me and I tell them, "Of course *I* haven't done the pro-gram. Would I look like this if I did? No, I'm waiting for my one-year mark. You see, after an employee has worked here a year, they can do the program for free. See those women over there, the ones pretending to be on business calls? The ones who look like super-models? They were just like me once. Then they did the program and now look at them."

I had the routine down. I signed a lot of customers. No, it wasn't the sales. It was the phones. All ringing at the same time, all day. All day. It made me, I'd look at the customer and feel compelled to tell the truth.

ROS. And what was that?

DONNA. That my supermodel co-workers were in grave danger. There was a phenomenon going on in Florida. It was hurricane season. And in strong winds, women like that were being swept up, blown away. People didn't realize it because they stay indoors and away from windows during storms. But if they just looked out the window they'd see it. Hundreds of skinny

DONNA. *(cont.)* super-model women flying through the air, being swept away by the wind.

It can be beautiful to watch.

(a beat)

You used to find me amusing.

(ROS *says nothing.)*

I could help you with the shop.

ROS. It's not a shop, it's a boutique.

DONNA. I could help you with the boutique.

ROS. Do you realize I'm the owner?

(DONNA *nods.)*

ROS. And you're thinking what? Sales? You think I'd allow you customer contact?

DONNA. No, I'd…anything…I'll sweep up or – whatever you ask me to do. You're in charge. Like – you're the older sister, not me.

ROS. That's the way it should have been.

(small pause)

ROS. I could show you what's it's like to have your life in order.

DONNA. Does that mean…?

ROS. For a little while.

DONNA. Really?

ROS. Your husband's dying, you lost your job, you have nowhere else to go. What did you expect I'd say?

DONNA. I expected you'd say no.

ROS. Look at me Donna. I'm strong now. I am structurally sound. You can not blow me over, you can not hurt me.

DONNA. That's never been my intention.

ROS. There's a futon in the office. You can stay there.

(Lights up on **KEITH** *in the office. He puts a vase back in its place. He notices* **DONNA***'s suitcase by the futon. He tries to ignore it but can't. He's drawn to it.)*

DONNA. So, the guy I just met. Keith.

ROS. What about him?

*(***DONNA** *raises her eyebrows suggestively.)*

ROS. We have a business together. A partnership. We'll probably get married at some point, after we've made the business work.

DONNA. How many?

ROS. How many what?

DONNA. How many children does he want?

*(***KEITH** *goes to the case and pops opens the snaps. He peeks inside.)*

DONNA. No, let me guess. Four. Same as you.

ROS. None, same as me.

DONNA. Come on.

*(***ROS** *says nothing.)*

I don't believe you.

*(***ROS** *says nothing.)*

Why?

(Lights down on McDonald's. **KEITH** *hears something and quickly closes the suitcase. He goes to the desk, pretending to work.* **ROBBY** *enters the flower shop office.* **KEITH** *keeps his head buried in his work.* **ROBBY** *punches in. He hangs his backpack up. He heads towards the basement.)*

KEITH. No one buys from fat people.

ROBBY. Okay.

KEITH. It makes them fat by association. People buy from people that affirm their own sense of identity. Or the identity they wish to have. Who wishes to be fat? No one.

KEITH. *(cont.)* And thus, no one buys from fat people. Which is another reason for Ros not to get pregnant and have a baby. Our business would suffer.

ROBBY. Got it.

(*A beat.* **KEITH** *lifts his head up.*)

KEITH. What are you standing there for? There are flowers downstairs.

(**ROBBY** *exits to the basement. When he's sure* **ROBBY** *is gone,* **KEITH** *heads back to suitcase. He hears something, and quickly goes back to the desk again.* **ROS** *and* **DONNA** *enter the office.*)

ROS. Keith?

KEITH. Working through lunch.

ROS. I'm taking Donna down to the basement. To set her up to work.

KEITH. Oh.

ROS. Short term.

DONNA. Thank you, Keith. I'm looking forward to working here.

KEITH. Uhh.

(**ROS** *and* **DONNA** *exit to the basement. If the steps are visible, they take* **DONNA** *longer to navigate.*)

(*Lights down on* **KEITH** *as* **ROS** *and* **DONNA** *reach the basement. The basement is dark, dank, dirty; completely unlike the bright ordered world of above.* **ROBBY** *sits at a long worktable, stripping and cutting a pile of roses.* **DONNA** *takes in her surroundings. She is out of breath.* **ROBBY** *can't help but look over.*)

ROS. Donna, this is Robby. Robby, this is my sister Donna. I know. No resemblance.

(to **DONNA***)*

Come here. These roses came in today. They need to be stripped of their thorns so they can go in a bouquet, here's a stripper. They also need to be cut since they've been out of water. Don't use a scissor it crushes the tubes, use this knife. Cut a diagonal to form a sharp end so we can stick it in an arrangement. After you cut it, put it in water. Watch.

(*ROS grabs a rose out of* **ROBBY***'s hand and demonstrates. There is both artistry and hostility to her demonstration.*)

DONNA. You're good at that.

ROS. Here's a chair, here's a stripper, here's a knife. There's an intercom over there. I'll buzz you when it's quitting time.

(*ROS goes to exit. She stops.*)

ROS. If you fuck with me I swear I'll throw you out on the street.

(*ROS exits up the stairs.* **DONNA** *and* **ROBBY** *briefly eye each other.* **DONNA** *holds out her hand for a rose.* **ROBBY** *gives her one.* **DONNA** *strips the thorns off her rose. She puts the stripper down, picks up the knife and cuts off the bottom of the stem as* **ROS** *demonstrated. Then she cuts another piece off the stem. Then another. Finally, only the flower's head is left.* **DONNA** *rips it apart with her hands. Pause.*)

DONNA. What the fuck are you staring at?

ROBBY. Nothing, I…nothing.

DONNA. Then give me another flower. And keep your eyes to yourself.

(**ROBBY** *quickly hands* **DONNA** *a rose. He takes one for himself.* **DONNA** *gets herself to calm down and strip the thorns off her rose. She picks up the knife and wills herself to cut the stem properly. She does. She places it in the bucket. She sighs with relief. The struggle has enervated her. She looks at* **ROBBY** *who quickly averts his eyes.*)

(**DONNA** *pulls her bag on her lap and digs into it, the sounds of a bag full of wrappers being jostled. It takes her a while to find what she wants.* **ROBBY** *glances over furtively. Finally* **DONNA** *finds it and pulls it out. A Snickers Bar. She senses* **ROBBY***'s gaze.*)

DONNA. You're doing it again.

ROBBY. I wasn't. I just glanced.

DONNA. At what? What's so damn interesting to look at? See? It's a candy bar. Would you like one?

ROBBY. Uh, okay.

DONNA. Staring-boy wants a candy bar. Okay, let me see what I have.

(looking into her bag)

I have Snickers, Snickers Cruncher, Twix, Twix Peanut Butter, Kit Kat, Chunky, PayDay, Mars, O'Henry, Three Musketeers, Charleston Chew (chocolate, vanilla and strawberry), Clark, Nutrageous, Butterfingers, Butterfingers BBs, Almond Joy, Mounds, Tootsie Roll, Junior Mints, Mr. Goodbar, Cadbury Caramello, Toffifay, Milk Duds, Whoppers, Goobers, Raisinettes, Milky Way, Milky Way Lite, Whatchamacallit, Heath Bar, Baby Ruth, 100 Grand, Nestle Crunch, Nestle Buncha Crunch, Zero, Crackel, Dove Bar, 5th Avenue, Rolo, York Peppermint Patty, Sugar Daddy, Sugar Babies, Reese's Peanut Butter Cups, Reese's Sticks, Reese's Fast Break, Reese's Crunchy Cookie Cups, Reese's Bites, Reese's Pieces, Skor, Hershey Bar, Hershey Bar with Almonds, Hershey Symphony, Hershey's Cookies and Cream, Hershey's Bites, Hershey's Hugs, Hershey's Special Dark Chocolate, Hershey's Kisses, Hershey's Kisses with Almonds, M&M's, Peanut M&M's, Almond M&M's, M&M's Dulce De Leche, M&M's Crispy, M&M's peanut butter.

*(**DONNA** looks up, stares directly at **ROBBY**. Long pause.)*

ROBBY. Kit Kat is good.

*(**DONNA** continues to peer at **ROBBY** a moment, then fishes into her bag and pulls out a Kit Kat. She tosses it to him. They each unwrap their candy. **DONNA** stares at **ROBBY**, sussing him out as he eats. **ROBBY** makes sure not to return her gaze.)*

*(**DONNA** looks around the basement. **ROBBY**, both daunted and fascinated, gets up his courage. He gives it a very, perhaps too eager attempt.)*

ROBBY. That's the back room.

    (**DONNA** *says nothing. A beat.*)

ROBBY. There's a big refrigerator back there, for the flowers. And a whole bunch of storage space.

    (**DONNA** *says nothing. A beat.*)

ROBBY. They keep a ton of stuff. Odds and ends, found objects, whatever Ros and Keith think they might use, for an event or whatever. Sometimes I think they've got one of everything in the world back there.

    (**DONNA** *again doesn't respond.* **ROBBY** *gives up and resumes working.*)

DONNA. You work down here all day?

ROBBY. *(eager to respond)* I do deliveries too. I alternate. But when I'm down here, I'm alone.

DONNA. What about Ros?

ROBBY. She rarely comes down. And Keith never does. He's got kind of – an aversion to it. Ros too, but Keith more so. It is pretty nasty down here.

DONNA. So why aren't *you* averse to it?

ROBBY. I don't know.

DONNA. Yes you do.

ROBBY. I – I don't know. I guess I feel more comfortable down here than I do up there. That sounds kind of crazy I know.

DONNA. No it doesn't.

ROBBY. You don't think so? If my brother saw this place and I said that, he'd have me locked up.

    (*small pause*)

ROBBY. So, you and Ros, I mean, I don't know but...it seems like...

DONNA. We've haven't seen or spoken to each other in six years.

ROBBY. Wow. Wow, I fantasize about not talking to my family for that long.

DONNA. But she took me in. *(amazed)* She took me in. There's hope.

(**DONNA** *pulls her bag up for another candy bar.*)

DONNA. Do you want another?

ROBBY. No.

DONNA. No?

ROBBY. No thank you.

DONNA. Why?

ROBBY. Why what?

DONNA. Why don't you want another one?

ROBBY. Uhh, I don't know, I –

DONNA. Think.

ROBBY. *(answering more definitely)* I feel full. That's why I don't want another one. The Kit Kat was filling.

DONNA. That's very logical of you.

ROBBY. I guess.

(**DONNA** *digs into her bag and pulls out a second candy bar. She tosses it at* **ROBBY.**)

DONNA. Sometimes you need to explode an existing logic, in order to create a new one.

(**ROBBY** *is struck by this. Almost in a trance, he unwraps the candy bar and eats it.* **DONNA** *watches. From the intercom comes* **ROS** ' *voice.*)

ROS. *(on intercom)* Robby?

(**ROBBY,** *eating, doesn't answer.*)

ROS. *(on intercom)* Robby come up. I need you to make a run.

(*Still transfixed,* **ROBBY** *rises. The lights go down on the flower shop as* **ROBBY** *moves downstage, sits in a chair and pretends to be driving the flowershop truck. He leans out the "window."*)

ROBBY. FUCK YOU TOO! YEAH? WELL I'LL JAM MY THUMB IN YOUR EYE SOCKET AND SCRAMBLE YOUR FUCKING BRAINS!

(**ROBBY** *gives a goofy smile. Some applause and hollers.*
ROBBY *pulls out a drink, takes a sip then looks front
again, one hand casually on the "wheel." He still pretends to be driving, free and loose, delighting in his new
discovery.*)

ROBBY. Logic tells you,
Don't drive right behind him,
no,
that sure isn't right.
Logic tells you,
try not to blind him
oops
guess I'm flashing my brights.
Logic tells you,
don't swerve out around him,
please,
and don't cut him off.
Logic tells you,
you should recycle
but it's only backwash.

(*He finishes his drink, holds the bottle up. Lights come
up on* **DONNA** *holding a flower pot.*)

ROBBY. Here's to logic!

(*He mimes tossing the bottle out the window. Applause –
and the sound of glass breaking as* **DONNA** *purposefully
throws the pot down and watches* **KEITH**'s *reaction.*)

Scene Five

(*The office. The broken pot at* **DONNA**'s *feet.* **KEITH**
stands, staring at the shards, traumatized. **ROS** *enters.*)

ROS. What was that?

KEITH. She – she broke a pot. It's broken. It's all in pieces.
Shattered. On the floor.

DONNA. I'll pay for it.

ROS. That's right you will.

(ROS gets a broom and a dustpan and hands it to DONNA. She exits back to the bathroom. KEITH can only stare at DONNA, a moth drawn to the fire. Pause.)

(DONNA holds out the dustpan. KEITH can't help but take it. He bends down, but continues to stare up at DONNA, unable to take his eyes off her as she hovers above him. DONNA sweeps the pieces into the pan. Only when she steps back can KEITH rise with the pan. He continues to stare at DONNA. ROS re-enters.)

DONNA. *(to ROS)* It was an accident. The pot.

ROS. We're closed now. Do *not* answer the door and do *not* answer the phone.

DONNA. What if they call about Scott?

ROS. You gave this number? We have an answering service. I'll check the messages in the morning.

(to KEITH who still holds the dustpan)

Are you ready honey?

KEITH. *(still staring at DONNA)* For what?

ROS. For us to go home.

KEITH. *(finally turning to ROS)* Both of us?

(ROS glances nervously at DONNA.)

ROS. Of course, silly.

(trying to spell it out without DONNA catching on)

And Donna will stay here on the futon.

KEITH. Oh. Right. Okay.

ROS. *(to DONNA)* We'll see you tomorrow.

(ROS takes the dustpan from KEITH and empties it into the garbage. She exits, followed by KEITH. He turns back for one more look at DONNA as he goes.)

(DONNA, now alone, sits on the futon and takes a piece of candy from her bag. She eats.)

Scene Six

(Later. DONNA sits in the same position. A few candy wrappers on the floor. The phone rings. Four times then stops. It rings again. DONNA, sits, listening to the phone ring, the sound loud and echoing, just as she described it to ROS.)

(Lights fade on DONNA and come up on ROS and KEITH at home. ROS sits, the phone receiver to her ear. KEITH enters carrying a blanket and pillow.)

ROS. Good, she's not picking up.

(hangs up)

I'll try again in a few minutes. To make sure.

KEITH. Good idea.

(pause)

KEITH. Well, guess I'll – go to sleep now.

ROS. *(rising)* Darling, why don't you take the bedroom.

KEITH. No. You go ahead.

(a beat)

ROS. Unless of course…I mean, if you want…we could –

KEITH. I thought you're going to call again.

ROS. Yes. I will. I'm going to.

KEITH. Glad to see you're covering all the bases.

ROS. Making my list, checking it twice.

KEITH. *(affectionate though forced)* You're a good – business partner.

(KEITH stands frozen a moment, then exits. ROS sits alone a beat, then turns back to the phone and dials again.)

Scene Seven

*(Morning. **ROBBY** sitting with **DAVID** on a bench. **DAVID** is observing a schoolyard, thumbing notes into a Blackberry. **ROBBY** eagerly observes **DAVID**.)*

DAVID. Sorry I was late. I had to deal with my car.

ROBBY. Your car?

DAVID. Window was smashed. Driver's side. You believe that?

*(**ROBBY** doesn't answer.)*

DAVID. I cover the fundamentals. *One*: leave the glove compartment open, *two* –

ROBBY. David, I know the checklist. That was Tuesday's test. I passed it.

DAVID. A little review wouldn't hurt you.

*(**DAVID** turns back to the playground, as does **ROBBY**.)*

I cover the fundamentals.

*(**DAVID** sees something noteworthy. He types it in.)*

Where's yours?

ROBBY. I have it.

DAVID. Let's see.

*(**ROBBY** fishes out an identical Blackberry, shows it to **DAVID**.)*

DAVID. You read the manual?

ROBBY. Yes I read the manual.

DAVID. Show me something.

*(**ROBBY** holds it up for **DAVID**.)*

ROBBY. Appointments. Meet David, meet David, meet David, meet David.

*(**ROBBY** starts to put the Blackberry away.)*

DAVID. Keep it out.

*(**ROBBY** does. **DAVID** turns back to the playground. **ROBBY** continues to observe **DAVID**, waiting for the right moment. Then...)*

ROBBY. There's a new employee. At the flower shop. Sister of the owner.

DAVID. Oh yeah?

ROBBY. Yeah. She's kind of…interesting.

DAVID. Interesting, huh?

ROBBY. Yeah. Yeah, she…interests me. The day I met her, she said something that…I don't know, it really…

DAVID. Articulate.

ROBBY. I'm trying.

DAVID. They would've taught you that in college.

ROBBY. *(meaningfully)* Sometimes you need to explode an existing logic in order to create a new one.

(*The* HOMELESS MAN *enters [unseen to them.])*

DAVID. What the hell is that supposed to mean?

ROBBY. It means…you know…like, like your car. You know. You sealed it up. It was secure –

DAVID. And empty. Don't forget that. That's important.

ROBBY. But the window got smashed anyway. You see?

(**DAVID** *considers a beat.*)

DAVID. You think I should leave the doors unlocked?

(*sees the* **HOMELESS MAN**)

Risk some guy like that getting in. Shit. Shit.

ROBBY. What?

DAVID. I looked at him. I shouldn't have looked at him.

(*The* **HOMELESS MAN** *approaches* **DAVID** *and* **ROBBY**. *He stands before them. He lifts his shirt.*)

HOMELESS MAN. This is a map of Jesus.

(*He points to the spot on his ribs.*)

And this is where I feed him.

ROBBY. *(in unison with above)* And this is where I feed him.

(*The* **HOMELESS MAN** *puts his shirt down and stares at* **ROBBY**. **ROBBY** *digs into his pocket and gives him some change. The* **HOMELESS MAN** *takes it but remains. He draws a large "9" in the air with his finger.*)

HOMELESS MAN. Number nine.

> (*He draws another.*)

Number nine.

> (*He draws a third.*)

Number nine.

> (*He exits.* **DAVID** *still stares down at the ground.*)

ROBBY. He's gone.

> (**DAVID** *looks up and checks to make sure, then turns to* **ROBBY**.)

DAVID. Are you nuts?! Have you completely lost your mind?!

ROBBY. I've seen him before.

DAVID. (*beside himself*) So what!? Jesus Robby! Type this in. Type it.

ROBBY. What?

DAVID. You never look at them. Never. And you certainly don't talk to them. Type it.

> (**ROBBY** *thumbs the keys of his Blackberry.* **DAVID** *calms down and watches the playground. He inputs notes into his Blackberry.* **ROBBY** *finishes, watches* **DAVID**.)

ROBBY. What are you doing?

DAVID. Observations. We're on the waitlist for this elementary school.

> (**DAVID** *continues to input.*)

ROBBY. Don't you need a child to be on the wait list?

DAVID. Are you kidding? The average wait for this school is seven years. That's one. *Two*: even when your number comes up, it only means you can apply. That's why I'm here. To find something useful – for the personal statement. For this, or any of the five schools I'm observing.

> (**ROBBY** *watches* **DAVID**.)

ROBBY. David I…

DAVID. (*still facing forward*) What?

ROBBY. I think I can help you.

(**DAVID** *inputs some detail he observes in the playground.* **ROBBY** *turns front, joining* **DAVID** *in watching the playground. They both hold their Blackberrys, looking out. The school bell rings.*)

Scene Eight

(*The sound of the bell bridges the scenes, now becoming more like a doorbell.* **DONNA** *sleeps on the futon in the flower shop office. The bell rings again.* **DONNA** *rouses.*)

(*The bell continues to ring, insistently.* **DONNA** *sits up, unsure of what to do. Finally, as the bell rings and rings, she rises and exits to the front of the store.*)

Scene Nine

(*The empty office, a bit later.* **ROS** *enters, expecting to see* **DONNA**. *A familiar dread comes over her as she sees* **DONNA** *is absent. The phone rings.*)

ROS. Good morning. Ros-Farmer Floral Design.

Scene Ten

(*Seated at her table,* **DONNA** *orders breakfast.* **ROBBY** *enters unseen and watches her.*)

DONNA. 2 Egg McMuffins, 2 Sausage McMuffins, 2 Bacon Egg and Cheese Biscuits, 2 Ham, Egg and Cheese Breakfast Bagels, 2 Spanish Omelette Breakfast Bagels, 2 Large Hash Browns, 2 Sausage McGriddles Meals, 2 Big Breakfasts, 2 Hot Cakes and Sausage.

(**ROBBY** *is dumbstruck.* **ROS** *enters McDonald's.* **ROBBY** *sees her and quickly exits.* **ROS** *marches over to* **DONNA**'s *table and sits.*)

DONNA. *(confidently)* I knew you wouldn't want her to stand outside, get no service. She's a customer.

ROS. She called to thank you. To say she thought about your conversation all morning. Which alarmed me, of course.

(when **DONNA** *says nothing...)*

So I ask her what changes she's come up with. Gwyneth Pierpont makes it a habit of getting hysterical then demanding rash changes. And there was no telling, after talking to you what was coming.

DONNA. She didn't change anything.

ROS. No.

DONNA. I talked her down.

ROS. That's what she said.

DONNA. And?

ROS. And that she wouldn't dream of changing another thing. Words I never thought I'd hear from her mouth. How? How did you get her to say that?

DONNA. Charm.

(a beat)

Guess you don't have to throw me out on the street.

(a beat)

Did she tell you? What her concern was?

ROS. No.

DONNA. Her bridesmaids. Their bouquets.

ROS. Her bridesmaids bouquets? They're exquisite. A half dozen red roses in a hand wrap made from the tulle of her Grandmother's wedding veil. The roses unopened, somewhere between bud and bloom. While Gwyneth's roses will be fully open; the bride on her wedding day, in full bloom.

DONNA. Pretty.

ROS. Perfection. What could possibly be wrong with it?

DONNA. Maybe I shouldn't say. I really shouldn't have opened the door in the first place.

ROS. Donna.

DONNA. She's terrified her bridesmaids will upstage her. A procession of tight little bodies with their tight little rosebuds. She's terrified that all the men, including her fiancé, will ogle them, and imagine what it's like inside their flowers, inside those tight, red buds.

(*A beat.* **ROS** *and* **DONNA** *break out laughing.*)

ROS. (*as their laughter trails off*) What?

DONNA. Nothing.

ROS. Donna, I know that look. What?

DONNA. Nothing.

(*a beat*)

When I let your client in this morning, she expected that someone would be there.

(**ROS** *says nothing.*)

She said one of you is always there. 24-hours.

ROS. (*sharply*) There's a reason for that.

DONNA. I'm sure.

ROS. One you wouldn't understand.

DONNA. Okay.

ROS. Our business comes first. That's the rule.

(*sharply*)

I told you not to open the door.

DONNA. Ros –

ROS. Didn't I?

DONNA. I did right this morning.

(*when* **ROS** *says nothing...*)

I have done nothing wrong since I got here. Nothing.

ROS. That's not what I hear.

DONNA. What do you hear?

ROS. That you've had a little trouble cutting roses. That some of them don't quite survive your knife.

DONNA. Says who?

ROS. Says Robby. He keeps a strict record for us – of all the goings on down there.

(*A beat.* **ROS** *rises to exit.*)

Come to the shop when you're done.

(*She starts off.*)

DONNA. The boutique.

(**ROS** *stops.*)

DONNA. I'll come to the *boutique* when I'm done.

Scene Eleven

(*The office.* **KEITH** *kneels down beside the futon. He looks back toward the front room. Seeing the coast is clear, he pulls back the covers, looks at the mattress. He shakes his head at what he sees. He leans in and wipes the food crumbs he's discovered off the bed, and into his hand. He looks back toward the front room again. Then, with the collected crumbs in his hand, he reaches down inside his pants and deposits them there.*)

(**ROBBY** *enters and sees* **KEITH** *kneeling at the bed, his hand down his crotch.* **KEITH** *senses* **ROBBY**'*s presence. A beat.*)

KEITH. Donna's husband, the one who's dying? He's gay. Did you know that?

ROBBY. No, I didn't.

KEITH. She knew he was gay when they got married. They were friends. They never had sex.

ROBBY. Oh.

KEITH. How long do you think a man can last without having sex?

ROBBY. I don't know.

KEITH. I hold on to my testosterone. I keep it inside me. If it's drained, I'll lose power. People can smell that, they can sense it.

Scene Twelve

(The basement. A bit later. **ROBBY** *sits at the work table, with a clipboard, recording the cut flowers in the bucket before him.* **DONNA** *enters.)*

ROBBY. Hi.

*(***DONNA*** goes right toward* **ROBBY.** *She grabs the open knife from the table and holds it against* **ROBBY**'s *neck.)*

DONNA. You little snitch.

ROBBY. She insisted. She said there must have been something. It couldn't have been perfect. So I told her.

DONNA. That what? That I'm intentionally destroying flowers? That I'm sabotaging things down here?

ROBBY. No, no. I said you miscut a few. That was it.

*(***DONNA*** stares him down.)*

DONNA. I need her. Do you understand me? I need her.

ROBBY. I'm sorry. I…I won't say another word.

*(***DONNA*** continues to stand over him, then tosses the knife back on the table and sits. A beat.)*

*(***DONNA*** takes a flower, cuts it properly.* **ROBBY** *cautiously resumes his counting. Silence as they work.)*

ROBBY. I saw you at McDonald's this morning.

DONNA. And? Do you have something to say about that?

ROBBY. No. Yeah.

DONNA. Well go ahead. Spit it out. You think I haven't heard it before.

ROBBY. No, I just – your order.

DONNA. Right.

ROBBY. I listened to you order and it, it –

DONNA. Right.

ROBBY. It sounded like a poem.

(A beat. **DONNA** *is taken aback.)*

DONNA. What?

ROBBY. Like you were slamming.

(**DONNA** *is speechless.*)

ROBBY. Do you know what slamming is?

(**DONNA** *shakes her head.*)

ROBBY. It's kind of poetry in performance. You know, sometimes it's improvised, sometimes not. I, uh, do a little of it myself at this place around the corner.

(*sheepishly*)

Anyway, when I heard you order, that's what I thought of. It was really...I don't know...inspiring.

(**DONNA** *giggles to herself.*)

ROBBY. You should try it sometime. Slamming. I was planning on, you know, dropping by there tonight.

(**DONNA** *looks utterly baffled.*)

ROBBY. I mean, in case you wanna – join me.

(*pause*)

DONNA. Do they serve food there?

ROBBY. Yeah. Yeah, they totally do.

(*A beat. The intercom sounds.*)

ROS. (*on intercom*) (*sing-song*) Yoo-hoo. This is your boss Ros speaking. Interrupting the hard work that I know is going on down there. Robby?

ROBBY. Yes, Ros.

ROS. (*on intercom*) Come on up. There are some beautiful arrangements up here, and they're ready for delivery.

ROBBY. Yeah, okay, coming up.

(**ROBBY** *goes to exit. Stops.*)

ROBBY. (*to* **DONNA**, *proudly*) I smashed the driver's side window of my brother's car.

(*exits*)

(*Lights down, then up on the office, later.* **KEITH** *and* **ROS**, *ready to leave for the day, wait for* **DONNA** *to get up the stairs.*)

KEITH. Jesus Christ, you think it was the fucking stairway to heaven she was climbing.

(**DONNA** *enters from downstairs.*)

DONNA. *(catching her breath)* Sorry to keep you waiting.

ROS. *(starts to go)* I'll lock the basement door.

KEITH. *(terrified of being alone with* **DONNA***)* No. Let me. I'll do it.

(*He quickly exits to the stairs.* **ROS** *turns to take care of last minute business.*)

DONNA. *(whispering)* Ros.

(*no answer*)

Ros.

ROS. What?

(**DONNA** *gestures for her to come over to her.* **ROS** *hesitates then does.*)

DONNA. *(private)* I was thinking about this 24-hour thing. One of you staying here each night.

ROS. Donna –

DONNA. I think it shows your commitment. Sets this place apart. A nervous bride, a nervous mother, they wake up panicked, the middle of the night, and one of you is here to talk to. What other business can claim that?

ROS. *(pleased)* That's exactly what we thought, when we came up with the idea.

(**KEITH** *re-enters.*)

DONNA. *(in a lowered voice)* And if there's anything else you want to tell me – about the way things work here – I'd love to hear it.

(*waits a beat, whispers*)

I'll be at McDonald's.

(*She waits another beat.* **ROS** *says nothing.* **DONNA** *exits.*)

(**ROS** *moves to the office exit and looks offstage, watching* **DONNA** *leave the shop.*)

ROS. I think I'm rubbing off on her. I think I actually am. I knew it. I knew I could.

KEITH. She's eating dinner at McDonald's.

    (**ROS** *turns back to* **KEITH**.)

ROS. Should we join her?

KEITH. Are you – are you insane?

ROS. Kidding. Darling, it was a joke.

KEITH. It's not funny. Not at all. Just the thought of ingesting one of those fatty patties. Jesus. I need a bee-pollen.

    (looks for it)

Where the bottle? Where is it?

    (panicking)

WHERE'S MY FUCKING BEE POLLEN!

ROS. Right here honey.

    (She gives him the bottle. He grabs it from her, opens it, and removes a capsule and swallows it quickly.)

Scene Thirteen

    (spotlight on **ROBBY***)*

ROBBY. Yes.

You can take my order.

And

yes

is my order.

Because

No

is abstemious, it's empty, it's fear.

Yes

is open. Uncurling. Unabashed.

Fuck some. Fuck a little. How about all.

Are you ready for all?

    (Some applause and encouragement.)

(from the old commercial)

Big Mac, Fillet o' Fish, Quarter Pounder, French Fries.
Icy Coke, thick shake, sundae, apple pie.

(some applause)

I said yes. And yes again.

That's two yeses.

For two of each.

That's right.

Gimme two of each.

And make it to go.

The ark is waiting.

(A split of applause and heckling. **ROBBY** *goes to a table where* **DONNA** *sits. A selection of empty plates covers the table. She applauds vigorously for* **ROBBY** *as he sits.)*

DONNA. That was fabulous.

ROBBY. You think so?

DONNA. Yes. And yes again. Two yeses.

ROBBY. You want to try it?

DONNA. I don't think so.

ROBBY. I know you'd be good.

DONNA. I'd rather watch you.

ROBBY. You'll do better.

DONNA. This isn't the right crowd for me to stand up in front of.

ROBBY. Oh. Okay. Sorry.

DONNA. But I will try it. Sometime. I promise.

ROBBY. Okay.

DONNA. When it's the right crowd.

ROBBY. Sure.

    (pause)

ROBBY. *(bursting out with it)* I got kicked out of college. My family is flipped out about it. They think I'm totally unhinged.

DONNA. Are you?

ROBBY. *(pouring out of him)* I took a final. The kid behind me asks me what symbolism was. So I told him. The next day I get called in to face the Honor Code Board. A couple of kids reported us. The Board asks me, given the evidence, what action I thought they should take. I said, "fire the professor, promote me to faculty." I was serious. The kid spent an entire semester without learning what symbolism was. I aided the education of a peer. What's more honorable than that?

(**ROBBY** *looks at* **DONNA,** *anxiously awaiting her verdict.*)

DONNA. I think you did the right thing.

ROBBY. You do?

(**DONNA** *nods.* **ROBBY** *shouts to the heavens in celebration.*)

You're the first person who's told me that!

DONNA. I spread peanut butter on Ros' paintings.

ROBBY. *(laughs)* Really?

DONNA. It was part of a year-end showcase, at the institute where she was studying. There were art people there to see it.

(small beat)

Her paintings. All of them. They were of these hyper-crisp green apples in these perfect porcelain bowls. One had the title, 'After School Snack.' It was the bowl of apples on a kitchen table, with just *one* little girl in a pretty white dress looking at them. Ros and I used to have a game, we had a lot of them. In this one I'd give her a couple of dollars to buy a snack after school. And she would announce to me what she planned to get. Then I'd surprise her, come home with something to go with it. Whip cream for her hot chocolate. That sort of thing. A treat. One afternoon little Ros announces, apples. She wanted a bag of apples. So I went to the store and came home with a couple of jars of Jif. We ate it all, the apples and both jars of peanut butter. In a single sitting. Made quite a mess doing it.

She didn't invite me to her show. I just showed up. That's what I always did. When I sensed she needed me. I'd show up. So there I was, looking at this painting, 'After School Snack', without the peanut butter and without me. And I thought...I thought, this isn't art. This isn't what an artist does. The institute wasn't going to tell her that. They were too busy ripping her off. But the art people knew. They weren't paying much attention to her. Not compared to some of her classmates. So I went out and I bought some Jif, and while everyone was in another room listening to a guest speaker, I went to work. She got more attention after that.

(pause)

ROBBY. Crunchy or smooth? The peanut butter.

DONNA. You're a troublemaker.

ROBBY. So are you.

DONNA. No. Not anymore.

(a beat)

ROBBY. So...the flowershop, it's –

DONNA. *(definitive)* Stop. Stop right there.

ROBBY. Sorry.

(a beat)

DONNA. *(gets the better of her)* What about it?

ROBBY. *(bursting out of him again)* Keith says some really strange things to me. Like, that he has to hold on to his testosterone, for the sake of the business. Which he gave as the reason Ros shouldn't have a baby.

DONNA. Don't tell me that. You didn't tell me that. Shit! Shit! Why did you tell me that? All her life, she's wanted a baby. All her fucking life.

(more to herself)

Shit.

(pause)

ROBBY. *(A desperate and bizarrely cheery attempt to change the subject.)* My Dad has cancer. He wasn't going to tell me but he was bawling me out for getting expelled and it just came out. He hasn't told my brother.

DONNA. I'm sorry.

ROBBY. *(still cheery)* They caught it early. He might be okay. I guess if worse comes to worst, I know where to get flowers for a funeral.

(a beat)

DONNA. That's how I'd bury Scott. My husband. If it was me burying him. In flowers. A ton of them. In his coffin, on top of it. A mountain of them. Not a spec of dirt thrown on him. Only flowers.

(a beat)

Imagine if that's what I told Miss Pierpont this morning. Given her that image. She would have canceled her order on the spot.

ROBBY. And the store would come tumbling down.

DONNA. What does that mean?

ROBBY. Ros and Keith are totally flipped out about this wedding. They say the whole business is riding on it. The Pierponts are some big important family or something. If it doesn't go well next week, then…

DONNA. The store would come tumbling down.

ROBBY. Right.

*(He peers at **DONNA** then it occurs to him.)*

Hey, are you going to – ?

DONNA. No.

ROBBY. But you –

DONNA. No. Not anymore.

ROBBY. Okay.

(pause)

ROBBY. If you change your mind –

DONNA. I won't.

ROBBY. But if you do, I'd…

DONNA. You'd what?

ROBBY. *(mischievously)* I'd help you.

DONNA. Take me home.

ROBBY. Donna, I –

DONNA. Right now!

> (**DONNA** *stands. Then* **ROBBY** *gets up and they move forward out of the bar/restaurant space. They stand outside the flower shop. Silence.*)

ROBBY. Donna I…I'm really sorry if I –

DONNA. Theoretically. If we decided – to do something. To the wedding. How would we?

ROBBY. Ros and Keith are going to take the flowers for the ceremony to the church. A little while later, I take the flowers for the reception, to the club or whatever. After Ros and Keith split we could, theoretically, do whatever we wanted with those arrangements. Cut all the heads off, spray paint them black…

> *(He waits.)*

ROBBY. *(cont.)* You wouldn't have to decide…until then.

> *(pause)*

DONNA. I had a nice time with you tonight.

ROBBY. You did? Really? I did too.

> *(a beat)*

DONNA. Do you wanna – come inside?

ROBBY. Actually there's something I have to do. I have a date.

DONNA. Oh.

ROBBY. *(smiling)* With my brother's car.

> (**DONNA** *smiles. A beat.*)

ROBBY. I should go.

> *(He doesn't.)*

DONNA. Here. Wait. I have something for you.

> (**DONNA** *reaches into her bag. She goes to* **ROBBY**, *hands him a Kit Kat.*)

ROBBY. Thank you.

(They stand at close range.)

ROBBY. I should go.

(He doesn't.)

DONNA. Well…goodnight.

*(**DONNA** moves in toward **ROBBY**. He backs up, and continues backing up, practically across the stage.)*

ROBBY. Goodnight.

*(Lights go down on **DONNA**. **ROBBY** continues looking towards her.)*

*(Behind him, the **HOMELESS MAN** appears. Sensing something, **ROBBY** turns suddenly, sees him standing before him. **ROBBY** freezes. The **HOMELESS MAN** draws a nine in the air with his finger.)*

HOMELESS MAN. Number nine.

(He draws another)

Number nine.

(draws a third)

Number nine.

*(A beat. The **HOMELESS MAN** takes his hand and 'turns' the first nine 180 degrees, forming a six.)*

Six.

(He turns another)

Six.

(He turns the third)

Six.

*(He looks at **ROBBY**.)*

ROBBY. Come with me.

(blackout)

End of Act I

ACT II

Scene One

*(A police station waiting room. Day. **DAVID** paces, highly agitated. **ROBBY** enters.)*

DAVID. Robby.

ROBBY. What's going on?

DAVID. My car. My fucking car.

ROBBY. The window again?

DAVID. This morning, just as I go to open the door, I see something. I see something inside. Inside my car. Squirming around, moving. It was him.

ROBBY. Who?

DAVID. Him. That homeless guy. In my car. Inside my car. What did I tell you was the danger in leaving the doors unlocked? Robby, you need to know this.

ROBBY. The homeless. The homeless might crawl inside, spend the night.

DAVID. That's right. But I've learned now. And at least you'll benefit from my experience. Empty vessel, that's the way to go. But locked up. Empty vessel locked up.

ROBBY. David – ?

DAVID. If you're going to debate me, don't.

ROBBY. What happened to the homeless guy? Was he arrested? Is he here?

DAVID. No, dammit. I ran back to my apartment, I called the police, but by the time they got there he was gone. They told me I had to come down here to file a report. You'll help me describe him.

ROBBY. I'm not sure I can.

DAVID. You're the one who's gotten a good look at him.

ROBBY. I haven't really seen his face. Just his chest.

DAVID. So describe that.

ROBBY. Two nipples a belly button and some straggly hair.

DAVID. No distinguishing mark? No moles, nothing? Come on Robby, give me something.

ROBBY. He's, he's got some kind of wound below his rib-cage.

DAVID. Okay, okay. That's something. That could help them ID him.

ROBBY. Why not just let the guy go?

DAVID. He invaded my car.

(*gets up and paces again*)

Waiting, waiting, waiting. Do you know why? It's a non-emergency. That's what they tell me. This is not a non-emergency! I'll tell you that!

(*He sits.*)

This is not what I wanted for you today. I'm so sorry.

ROBBY. It's okay.

DAVID. I got the paper last night. The alternative one. I sat in bed circling jobs for you. Ones I thought you might like. But I forgot it. The paper. I didn't bring it with me. I'm really really sorry.

ROBBY. David, it's okay. I have a job.

DAVID. No, you have someplace you work. You do not have a job.

ROBBY. There's a wedding. A big one coming up. I can't leave.

DAVID. Why? Your name will be mud in the flower industry?

(**DAVID** *laughs. Then* **ROBBY** *does. A beat.* **DAVID** *gets up. Peers off into the station.*)

DAVID. (*getting up*) What the hell is taking so long. Are they completely useless here?

(*He calls out.*)

This is not a non-emergency!

ROBBY. *(chiming in)* – emergency!

(**DAVID** *turns to* **ROBBY***. They share a look then chant out in unison.* **ROBBY** *gets up on his chair.*)

ROBBY. This is not a non-emergency! This is not a non-emergency! This is not a non-emergency!

DAVID. This is not a non-emergency! This is not a non-emergency! This is not a non-emergency!

(*They laugh together. They stop as they notice someone coming. They turn to each other, then run out of the station together.*)

Scene Two

OFFSTAGE VOICE. That's right. That's right. Your abs have dialed 911.

(*Lights up on* **ROS** *taking a sculpting [exercise] class.*)

(*As the fitness instructor [offstage] talks,* **ROS** *goes through the various exercises on her mat – crunches, leg lifts, etc.* **DONNA** *sits at a table, watching* **ROS** *and eating a chocolate power bar.*)

FITNESS INSTRUCTOR. *(offstage)* It's a cellulite emergency and sweethearts, I'm here to offer EMS. Emergency muscle solidification. I will take that flab away. How do I do that? How Ros?

ROS. *(while crunching)* You sculpt.

FITNESS INSTRUCTOR. That's right. Like Michelangelo I believe that inside each formless block there is a beautiful sculpture struggling to burst out. I will help you burst out. We'll take away and take away and take away that cellulite, until your true form appears. Until you see – what truly lies within. Now give me ten more crunches!

(**ROS** *cranks out ten more, then collapses on her mat. She gets up, and joins* **DONNA** *at her table, out of breath.*)

DONNA. Wow, that was something.

ROS. I love this class. Michael is so inspirational.

DONNA. So this is how you lost all your weight? Michelangelo there helped you sculpt it all away.

ROS. That and abstinence.

DONNA. A combination.

(*A beat.* ROS *smiles.*)

DONNA. What?

ROS. You're eating a Power Bar.

DONNA. It's what they had at the counter. Thought I'd try it.

ROS. Much better for you than candy.

(*a beat*)

DONNA. I used to write you notes to get out of gym class.

ROS. In grade school.

DONNA. You begged me. I was good with a note. Got you excused three years in a row.

ROS. I hated being in the locker room, that's all. Those girls.

DONNA. I wrote notes for Scott, too. To get extra gym. He liked the locker room. Remember?

ROS. There was no message on the voicemail this morning.

(*A beat.* DONNA *catches* ROS *glancing at a man.*)

DONNA. Want me to get a number for you?

ROS. No.

DONNA. Why not?

ROS. Because I don't need you to.

DONNA. You always did.

ROS. Well, I don't anymore.

DONNA. So go ahead. You're not married.

ROS. Yet. I'm not married yet.

(*a beat*)

I can't believe you asked to come here with me. I'm glad.

DONNA. You are?

ROS. I know. It's not like you're working out, but – you're in the building. Watching me. Seeing how I do things. Which – I think you'd admit – has had a real influence on you.

DONNA. It has.

ROS. I knew it.

DONNA. More and more each day. It really makes me feel like…I should do something.

ROS. Donna, you keep following my lead, you get yourself on a program and who knows? Maybe we could even get you out and…dating.

DONNA. I am dating.

ROS. Come on.

DONNA. I'm dating someone.

ROS. Donna…okay. Who? Who are you dating? Does he have a name?

DONNA. I'll give you a hint. He works for you.

(*Applause bridges the scenes.*)

Scene Three

(**ROBBY** *enters. Night. Poetry slam. He holds a spark plug in his hand.*)

ROBBY. Spark plug.

Spark plug.

(*Lights come up on* **DAVID**, *talking to a mechanic [off-stage].*)

DAVID. The spark plugs?

ROBBY. They're under the hood.

They're on the inside.

DAVID. Why would a homeless guy steal my spark plugs?

ROBBY. They start the combustion process.

DAVID. Why is this happening?

ROBBY. Combustible.

DAVID. I do everything right.

ROBBY. Combustion.

DAVID. I do everything right!

*(Lights down on **DAVID**. Lights up on **DONNA**, standing and applauding for **ROBBY**. **ROBBY** smiles, bows for her.)*

Scene Four

*(**KEITH** in the office. He stands, cutting something carefully with a scissor. It's a candy bar wrapper. He cuts it open then gently smooths it out so it's flat against the table. Then he pulls off a piece of tape and puts it along the top edge of the wrapper. Then he pulls off another piece of tape and puts it along the bottom edge. He looks at it a beat then suddenly pulls his shirt all the way up and tapes the candy wrapper to his ribs.)*

*(**ROBBY** enters the office. Caught, **KEITH** quickly puts his shirt down. **ROBBY** pretends he's seen nothing. He rapidly tries to punch in and get down to the basement.)*

KEITH. What's it like?

ROBBY. Goin' really well. Things in really good shape down there.

KEITH. What's it like with her?

ROBBY. Who?

KEITH. Ros's sister.

ROBBY. Donna? She, she's good. She's really good.

KEITH. What about you know…her size, the blubber, the fat. How does that – affect things?

ROBBY. I guess she's a little slower sometimes. But really it doesn't stop her. She does anything you ask her to.

KEITH. *Anything?*

ROBBY. Oh yeah. You should come down sometime, check it out yourself.

KEITH. In the basement!

ROBBY. Oh, sorry. I know you don't go down there –

KEITH. While you're working!

ROBBY. Forget it. Forget I ever said anything. I'm going down right now. You know what we're doing down there, that's good enough.

(**ROBBY** *exits down to the basement.*)

KEITH. Ros!!

Scene Five

(*The basement.* **DONNA** *laughing, watching* **ROBBY**.)

DONNA. Do it again.

(**ROBBY** *places a bucket on the table. He strikes a pose, looking at it.* **DONNA** *unwraps a series of power bars and watches him.*)

ROBBY. It's fab. Faboo. Fabege. Fabulicious.

(**DONNA** *laughs.* **ROBBY** *holds out his finger.*)

DONNA. Oh, sorry.

ROBBY. Now picture this. The guests, seated at their tables, perfect strangers forced to converse with one another. So what's the easiest conversation for them to have? What is staring them directly in the face? What Donna?

DONNA. The table arrangements?

ROBBY. The single most important element at the wedding. That's what she said. So I told her, "Don't you worry Ros, they'll be safe with Donna and me."

DONNA. You did not.

ROBBY. (*impishly*) Given it any thought?

DONNA. (*serious*) Yes.

(**DONNA**, *finished unwrapping the third Power Bar, puts the three together, forming a sandwich. She eats.*)

ROBBY. Hey, I want to show you something.

(**ROBBY** *bends down and crawls under the table, close to* **DONNA**. *She reacts to his presence beneath her.*)

DONNA. What…what are you going to show me?

(*ROBBY still beneath her.*)

Do I just sit here?

(*ROBBY pops back out, with a box. He opens it.*)

ROBBY. The next phase of our work down here. The wedding rapidly approaching.

(*ROBBY pulls out a green spongy brick.*)

ROBBY. Voila.

DONNA. What is it?

ROBBY. This "Donna dear" is the building block of any arrangement. Oasis. It's foam, basically. You tape it to a plastic dish and soak it. So when you stick a cut flower in it, there's water for it to draw. That way it lasts a bit longer.

(*With a touch of fanfare, he presents it to* **DONNA** *and sits. She holds it in her lap. A beat.*)

DONNA. You're my oasis.

(*A beat.* **DONNA** *places her foot over* **ROBBY**'s, *and rubs along it.* **ROBBY** *sits frozen. Pause.*)

ROBBY. (*stiffly, awkwardly, barely able to get the words out*) It's going well with my brother.

DONNA. Oh yeah?

ROBBY. Yeah. I think, I think I'm having an effect on him. At the Police Station, he – he laughed. Haven't seen him do that in…I don't know.

(*Pause.* **DONNA**'s *foot still rubbing.*)

(**KEITH**'s *voice comes over the intercom, sounding very stilted.*)

KEITH. (*on intercom*) Uh, Robby. Robby, we would like to have you upstairs. It's…the display cases. Yes, the display cases. In the front. They need…cleaning.

ROBBY. Okay, Keith.

KEITH. (*on intercom*) So…please come up…that's it.

(**ROBBY** *and* **DONNA** *looks at each other. Awkwardness.* **ROBBY** *hesitates a beat, exits.*)

Scene Six

(**ROBBY** *enters the office.* **KEITH** *stares at him, scrutinizing.* **ROBBY** *starts toward the front room.*)

KEITH. Where are you going?

ROBBY. To clean the display cases.

KEITH. No. No, you stay right there.

ROBBY. I thought...

KEITH. Ros!

(**ROS** *enters.* **KEITH** *quickly exits.*)

ROS. *(smiles)* Hi Robby.

ROBBY. Hi.

ROS. Sit Robby.

(**ROBBY** *sits, as does* **ROS.**)

ROS. I'd like to ask you just a quickie little question.

ROBBY. What about?

ROS. About Donna. About you and Donna.

(trying to get him to say it)

About – what you two are doing?

ROBBY. *(panicked)* We're doing really good. Everything's in really good shape down there. We're ahead of schedule for the Pierpont wed –

ROS. Robby. That's not what I'm asking.

ROBBY. Oh. Oh.

ROS. Okay. How to put this? Robby, are you and Donna having – intercourse in the basement? Just a question.

ROBBY. No. No, we do our work downstairs. Both of us.

ROS. Of course you do. Of course. I knew the two of you couldn't be dating.

ROBBY. We are.

ROS. Excuse me?

ROBBY. I mean, we've, you know, gone out together. A couple of times.

ROS. On dates? You went out together on dates?

ROBBY. Yeah, I mean, I don't know. Yeah.

ROS. What did you do together?

ROBBY. What did we do?

ROS. Yes.

ROBBY. We went to a bar, you know, we had some food, I walked her back here.

ROS. And then?

ROBBY. And then what?

ROS. Did you kiss? Did you and Donna kiss?

ROBBY. No. No, we didn't.

ROS. Well, then that's not a date. Not if you didn't kiss.

ROBBY. But –

ROS. Stop right there. Stop. I will not have you indulge some – fantasy she has in that head of hers. That's not what she needs right now.

ROBBY. It's not a fantasy.

ROS. You haven't kissed. You haven't had intercourse.

(a beat)

Did she give you a blowjob?

ROBBY. This is –

ROS. She used to give a lot of them, you know. Boys in our high school flocked to her. She swallowed.

(when **ROBBY** says nothing)

There's been a lot of cum in that mouth of hers. Probably good you didn't kiss her. Donna devours is what they used to say. She doesn't date – she devours.

(A beat. **ROBBY** bolts out, freaked. A beat, **ROS** unsure of what to do. She moves to the office exit and looks off-stage, checking to see if **ROBBY**'s left the shop.)

(She turns back to the office, thinks. She impulsively goes to the intercom.)

ROS. Donna. Come up.

(ROS *quickly goes about straightening her desk.* DONNA *enters from downstairs, holding the piece of oasis.* ROS *continues straightening up, not turning to* DONNA. *A beat.*)

DONNA. What's wrong?

ROS. Nothing. We're closing early that's all.

DONNA. Why?

ROS. I thought it would be nice. We're ahead of schedule. And since Robby asked to go home early...

DONNA. Is he okay? Did something happen?

(ROS *stops arranging her desk, turns.*)

ROS. Donna.

DONNA. What?

ROS. He...Robby told me he was uncomfortable. Working downstairs. With you.

DONNA. He didn't say that.

ROS. He did.

DONNA. Bullshit.

ROS. Donna.

DONNA. You're lying.

ROS. I'm...fine. Fine. Then tell me, why did he request to work upstairs from now on?

DONNA. Did I take him from you, Ros? Is that what happened?

ROS. Please.

DONNA. It wouldn't be the first time.

ROS. He didn't tell me why he was so uncomfortable. Robby. So I wondered if maybe something happened between you?

DONNA. None of your business.

ROS. Maybe a misunderstanding? About your relationship?

(DONNA *says nothing.*)

ROS. Wouldn't be the first time.

*(**ROS** exits. **DONNA** sits slowly into the chair, the oasis on her lap. She looks down at it. Pause. The phone rings. **DONNA** doesn't move. Then, on the fourth ring, she quickly answers it.)*

DONNA. Robby?

Oh, sorry, I...

(Her face changes.)

This is she.

I see.

No, that's...

Yes.

Thank you.

*(She hangs up. Pause. **DONNA** unplugs the phone. Piece by piece, she dismantles it, as well as the base, the entire phone. Each piece she places carefully on the desk. She finishes dismantling the phone, surveys the litter of phone pieces before her. She picks one piece up and places it in her mouth. She swallows it. She takes a second piece, places it in her mouth, swallows. Lights fade on **DONNA.**)*

Scene Nine

*(Morning. **DAVID** squatting on a bench, outside, holding a pair of binoculars to his face. Perhaps he wears camouflage. **ROBBY** enters, unnoticed and watches him.)*

ROBBY. Is this another one of the schools on your list?

*(**DAVID** sees **ROBBY** and waves him over urgently.)*

(making a joke) Looking at little kids with binoculars, you could get arrested for that.

DAVID. I'm not looking at the children. I'm looking for him.

ROBBY. Who?

DAVID. Him. Him.

He knows the inside of my car, Robby. He knows.

(*hands* **ROBBY** *his binoculars*)

Here. Keep watch.

(**DAVID** *gets up and walks away from the bench, several feet behind [or to the side of]* **ROBBY**. *He undoes his pants and urinates.* **ROBBY** *turns.*)

ROBBY. What, what are you doing?

DAVID. I'm urinating.

ROBBY. David. We're in public.

DAVID. If you hold it in too long, you can do kidney damage. That's one. *Two*: it smells like urine over here already. *Three...*I'm done.

(**DAVID** *zips up and returns to the bench. He takes the binoculars back, resumes looking. A beat.* **ROBBY** *is freaked out.*)

DAVID. Hear about Dad?

ROBBY. Uhh...what about him?

DAVID. Two weeks from today. His last day of work. He set the date.

ROBBY. Oh.

(*a beat*)

DAVID. Two weeks from today – then I'm the patriarch.

Scene Ten

(*Same morning.* **KEITH** *stands frozen, staring down at what's left of the dismantled phone. After a beat or two,* **ROS** *enters. She stops, looks at* **KEITH**.)

ROS. What's wrong?

KEITH. Look.

(**ROS** *goes over to him.*)

KEITH. It's the phone.

ROS. What happened to it?

KEITH. She ate it.

> (*They both look at it.*)

She ate it.

DONNA (*offstage*) (*from the bathroom*) Ros? Ros?

ROS. Jesus Christ.

DONNA (*offstage*) Ros?!

ROS. I'm out here!

> (**ROS** *and* **KEITH** *continue to look at the phone pieces.*
> **DONNA** *enters, looking awful.*)

ROS. What did you do? What did you do?

DONNA. They called. Last night. About Scott.

ROS. So you ate the phone? I'll call 911.

DONNA. No.

ROS. Donna –

DONNA. I threw it up.

ROS. This is unbelievable. Even for you.

DONNA. Scott's dead.

ROS. I heard you.

I think you should go to a meeting.

KEITH. What kind of meeting do you go to when you eat a phone?

> (**ROS** *goes and gets a Yellow Pages out.*)

DONNA. Ros?

ROS. I'll find the closest chapter.

> (*to* **KEITH**)

Overeaters Anonymous.

DONNA. Would you come with me? Ros?

ROS. What? *I* don't need to go.

DONNA. Please.

ROS. I...I'd rather not be around those people.

DONNA. Why? Why?

ROS. Because I'm not one of them.

DONNA. You were.

ROS. *(to* **KEITH**, *firmly)* No. I was never like that.

DONNA. Yes you were.

ROS. *(to* **KEITH***)* Never.

DONNA. My husband died.

ROS. Never.

DONNA. My husband died!

ROS. HE WASN'T A REAL HUSBAND!

> *(silence)*

ROS. I have a business to run. I can't just pop out at any time during the day.

DONNA. A business? A fucking morgue. That's what this is. You put your pretty little flowers in whatever pretty little arrangement you want. It doesn't matter. They're dead. All of them.

ROS. Talking nonsense. As usual.

DONNA. What happens to a flower, when you cut it from its roots? What? It dies. That's what happens. The moment it's cut – Good. As. Dead. And if I could do it again, that's what I'd tell Gwyneth Pierpont. Cancel your order Gwyneth! Hurry! These arrangements, they're not for a wedding. THEY'RE FOR A FUCKING FUNERAL!

> *(A beat.* **ROS** *runs out.)*

KEITH. *(panicked to be alone with* **DONNA***)* Ros?

> *(calling after her)*

Ros? Ros, where are you going?!

> *(He slowly turns back to* **DONNA***. They look at each other. While continuing to stare at* **KEITH***,* **DONNA** *reaches for her bag. She pulls a candy bar from it. She peels the wrapper halfway down. She gives the candy bar a blow job. She does it with relish and takes an excruciatingly long time. Pause.)*

(**DONNA** *goes to* **KEITH**. *He wilts into his chair as she approaches.* **DONNA** *stands before him.*)

KEITH. *(breathless, sexual)* You're disgusting. Revolting. Atrocious. Foul. Hideous. Detestable. Rank. Appalling. Beastly.

(**DONNA** *takes the end of her melted candy bar and smears it slowly around* **KEITH**'s *mouth.*)

(*She finishes, stands over him a moment, then exits.*)

(**KEITH** *alone, unable to move. Slowly, he sticks his tongue out and runs it along the chocolate around his mouth.*)

Scene Eleven

(*Perhaps the following two tenets overlap with* **KEITH** *alone, above.*)

A VOICE. *(offstage)*
WE.
1. Admit that we are powerless over food – that our lives have become unmanageable.
2. Believe that a Power greater than ourselves can restore us to sanity.

(*Lights up on* **DONNA** *at an O.A. meeting, listening to the speaker [offstage.]* **DONNA** *faces front looking ill, tired and angry.*)

O.A. SPEAKER.
3. Make a decision to turn our will and our lives over to the care of God as we understand Him, or Her.

(**ROBBY** *enters. He sits next to* **DONNA**. *She doesn't look at him.*)

O.A. SPEAKER.
4. Make a searching and fearless moral inventory of ourselves.
5. Admit to God, to ourselves and to another being the exact nature of our wrongs.

ROBBY. I'm sorry.

O.A. SPEAKER.

6. Are entirely ready to have God remove all these defects of character.

DONNA. For what?

O.A. SPEAKER.

7. Humbly ask Him, or Her, to remove our short-comings.

ROBBY. For your loss. I, I heard.

O.A. SPEAKER.

8. Make a list of all persons we have harmed and become willing to make amends to them all.

9. Make direct amends to such people wherever possible.

(**ROBBY** *turns to* **DONNA**. *He wants to say more, but doesn't.*)

O.A. SPEAKER.

10. Continue to take personal inventory and when we were wrong, promptly admit it.

(**DONNA** *laughs to herself, mockingly.*)

11. Seek through prayer and meditation to improve our conscious contact with God as we understand Him, or Her. Praying only for knowledge of His, or Her, will for us and the power to carry that out.

DONNA. (*puts her hands in 'prayer' position*) I'm praying.

O.A. SPEAKER.

12. Having a spiritual awakening as the result of these Steps, we try to carry this message and practice these principles in all our affairs.

Applaud yourselves. Applaud yourselves. Okay. Now it's time to hear testimony. Let us start with our new guests. Please, I see a few new faces out there. If you feel able, it's a wonderful first step.

(**DONNA** *raises her hand.*)

DONNA. (*to* **ROBBY**) This is the right crowd.

O.A. SPEAKER. Yes, thank you. In the back there.

*(**DONNA** stands.)*

DONNA. My name's Donna. Last night I ate a telephone.

*(As **DONNA** continues, it sweeps her away, gaining an angry momentum.)*

But it's still ringing inside me.

Like a dinner bell.

It tells me…it tells me it's time.

To eat.

And eat. And eat.

Everything.

Flesh from animals. Fruit from trees. Plants from soil.

The soil itself I'll swallow.

And all that's in it. Rocks, worms, beetles.

I will swallow an entire tree. Bark, leaves, roots.

I will eat all things, animate and inanimate.

I will become

a cauldron.

A cauldron with a special brew

being made.

Made from every bit of the world.

I will ingest every bit of the world. Ingest it until I become it.

Round. Full. Mother Earth.

From *me* will come creation.

O.A. SPEAKER. Uh… thank you. Anyone else?

*(**DONNA** steps back and sits. **ROBBY** is dumbfounded, in awe.)*

ROBBY. That was amazing. You slammed, you just totally slammed. Where'd you get that?

DONNA. What the fuck are you doing here?

ROBBY. Donna –

DONNA. You denied me.

ROBBY. No, I didn't, I –

DONNA. I decided.

ROBBY. You decided? You mean –

DONNA. The wedding.

(*a beat*)

Did you hear what I said?

ROBBY. Yeah, I…

DONNA. What? You having second thoughts?

ROBBY. Things are just – they're getting a little – out of hand. I mean –

DONNA. You coward. You scared little boy. Too frightened to take action. Too frightened to follow through. I knew you didn't have it in you. I knew it. From the first moment I met you.

(*DONNA exits. ROBBY sits alone, lost, looking straight ahead. A beat, then…music. Something anarchic.*)

(*ROS enters. She gets down on the floor and does crunches. A lot of them, very fast.*)

(*KEITH enters, a different playing area. He has a shopping bag. He reaches in and takes out a candy bar. He tears it open and puts it down his pants. He reaches into the bag, takes out another and does the same, tears it open and shoves it down his pants. He continues doing it.*)

(*The* **HOMELESS MAN** *enters. He lifts his shirt. It's* **ROBBY**'s *call to action. He rises, picks the chair up over his head and runs with it offstage.*)

(*The sounds of broken glass and metal.* **ROBBY** *attacking* **DAVID**'s *car.*)

(*DAVID enters. He has his binoculars and is searching frantically. He spots the* **HOMELESS MAN**, *stops.* **DAVID** *lets out a scream and runs at him and tackles him to the ground.*)

DAVID. (*call of the wild*) I AM THE PATRIARCH! I AM THE PATRIARCH!

(*DAVID raises his binoculars, ready to bring them down on the* **HOMELESS MAN**'s *head when* **ROBBY** *re-enters, carrying the steering wheel from* **DAVID**'s *car. He sees* **DAVID** *on top of the* **HOMELESS MAN**.*)

ROBBY. David!

DAVID. Robby it's okay! We're safe now! I got him! I got h –

(**DAVID** *looks up and sees* **ROBBY** *holding his steering wheel.*)

DAVID. That's my steering wheel.

(**ROBBY** *drops the wheel and runs.* **DAVID** *turns slowly and looks back down at the* **HOMELESS MAN**. *Blackout.*)

ACT III

Scene One

(Day. The basement. On the floor is a pile of McDonald's wrappers, cups, meal boxes. **DONNA** *sits at the table, eating and working on an arrangement. She covers the oasis that holds the flowers with pieces of moss. When she finishes, she places the whole thing into a clay pot.* **ROS** *comes down the stairs, surveys the mess. Pause.)*

ROS. I guess you never made it to O.A.

*(***DONNA*** takes a big bite of a burger. She chews ostentatiously, with an open mouth.)*

ROS. I really thought you were making progress.

DONNA. I am. Look.

*(***ROS*** goes over and peers into the flower pot. As she does,* **ROBBY** *enters, unnoticed. He ducks back onto the stairs.)*

DONNA. Did it all by myself. The rest of you upstairs and all. Except Keith. He seems to be missing again today. Where is he?

ROS. He's out.

DONNA. Out?

ROS. Home.

DONNA. Again? And the day before the big wedding?

ROS. I'm doing everything myself.

DONNA. That's odd.

ROS. He won't leave the apartment. Why?

*(***DONNA*** says nothing.* **ROS** *grabs a burger away from her.)*

ROS. Why won't he leave the apartment?

DONNA. *(pointed, imitating* **ROS***) Maybe he's not a real partner.* Step four: "Make a searching and fearless inventory of yourself."

(She takes another showy bite of food.)

ROS. Step eight: "Make a list of the people you've harmed and become willing to make amends to them."

DONNA. Good one. Go ahead.

ROS. You have a lot more to be sorry about than I do. Years worth of it.

DONNA. No.

ROS. *No?* You are completely out of your mind. After every-thing…after everything, and still I take you in, try to help you.

DONNA. Ha!

ROS. Step two: "Believe someone greater than yourself can restore you to sanity."

DONNA. A *Power* greater than ourselves. As in Mother Earth. As in God.

ROS. Whatever.

DONNA. *You* are not a Power greater than me.

ROS. Oh no? Look at me. Look what I've done for myself. By force of my own will.

DONNA. *(pounds the table)* You are not saner than me!

ROS. Then where's Robby? Huh? Where's your boyfriend? The one you never kissed? How come he's not down here?

(A beat. **DONNA** *does not reply.* **ROS** *starts to exit, vic-torious. As she gets to the stairs,* **ROBBY** *quickly enters. Pretending he's just arrived.)*

ROS. Speak of the devil.

ROBBY. All done.

ROS. Well then, let's you and I go upstairs and we'll chat about what's next.

(**ROS** *starts off.* **ROBBY** *stays.*)

ROS. Robby?

ROBBY. I'm finished upstairs.

ROS. Don't worry. I'll give you something else.

(**ROBBY** *goes and sits at the table.*)

ROBBY. This is where my work is.

(*more for* **DONNA**)

This is where I want to be.

(**DONNA** *turns to* **ROS**, *smiles.*)

ROS. Get that stupid smile off your face. Do you know why he's down here?

DONNA. Why?

ROS. I told him –

ROBBY. I'm not one of the boys from your high school.

(*a beat*)

DONNA. You jealous bitch.

ROS. He had a right to know.

(**DONNA** *throws a handful of fries at* **ROS**. *A beat.*)

ROS. I expect you'll clean those up.

(**DONNA** *throws another handful of fries.*)

ROS. If you do that again, I will fire you both.

(*She waits.*)

Very good. Now get back to work!

(**ROS** *exits.* **DONNA** *and* **ROBBY** *alone, they turn to each other.*)

Scene Two

(Lights up on **ROS***, in her and* **KEITH***'s apartment, pacing, with a phone in her hand.* **KEITH** *sits nearby in a chair, staring off into space, catatonic.)*

*(***ROS** *listens. No answer. She hangs up. She waits an impatient beat or two then picks up and dials again.)*

ROS. Making sure.

(She listens again, hangs up again. Pent up, she doesn't know what to do with herself.)

(Suddenly she looks out, a faint idea.)

ROS. Keith?

*(***KEITH** *doesn't move or speak.)*

ROS. Keith.

(Nothing. Finally she turns and looks at him, desperate for him.)

ROS. KEITH!!

*(***KEITH** *turns his head slightly toward her.)*

ROS. We need to talk about tomorrow.

Scene Three

(Late afternoon. The flower shop basement. **DONNA** *sits, holding an open knife, a finished arrangement on the table. She contemplates it, running her knife along the flowers, pokes at a stem, perhaps prunes a little leaf off. The intercom sounds. Lights come up on* **ROS** *in the office, at the intercom.)*

ROS. Donna? Donna?

*(***DONNA** *doesn't answer.)*

Donna, I'm going to be leaving in a minute...I'm going extra early. In case there's any last minute...anything.

(attempting levity)

You know Gwyneth.

(a beat, then genuine)

Any advice before I go. Any words of wisdom?

(silence)

Donna...I want to say something. About the other day. About what I said.

DONNA. Never too late to add insult to injury.

ROS. I'm sorry.

DONNA. Spare me. You think I can't take it? Come on, almighty one, spit it out.

ROS. *(Deliberately. Spelling it out.)* I mean I am sorry for what I said. About Scott.

(a beat, then seizing the opening)

And I'm also – sorry about Scott.

(pause)

DONNA. Me too.

(a beat)

Thank you.

ROS. You're welcome.

(pause)

DONNA. One of us apologizing. That's a benchmark.

ROS. True.

DONNA. Better be careful, might be habit forming.

ROS. I'll risk it. Sorry. There, did it again. I'm living on the edge.

DONNA. And what's that one for?

ROS. Put it in the bank.

(a beat)

I'm just waiting for Robby. He's almost done loading for the ceremony.

DONNA. What about Keith?

ROS. He's at home.

*(**ROBBY** enters the office.)*

ROBBY. The stuff's in the van. You're all set.

ROS. You going downstairs now?

ROBBY. Yeah. Donna and I will put all the table arrangements into their crates. Then we'll load 'em up.

(He waits.)

ROS. Okay then.

*(**ROBBY** exits to the basement. **ROS** speaks through the intercom again.)*

ROS. Robby's headed down. So I'll – I'll be going now.

DONNA. Ros?

ROS. Yes?

DONNA. You asked me for my advice.

ROS. I used to rely on it.

(a beat, difficult to ask)

You handled Gwyneth so well so...I guess I wondered – what would Donna do, what would Donna say if...if for – some reason – it doesn't all go exactly as planned.

DONNA. *(thinks, then...)* I'd make something up. Something outlandish. More fun that way.

*(**ROS** smiles, as does **DONNA**. **ROBBY** enters.)*

DONNA. That's my advice.

ROS. Thank you.

*(**ROS** releases the intercom. As **ROBBY** talks, **ROS** goes back briefly to the stairs then returns, exiting out the front of the store.)*

ROBBY. You know what would make that arrangement look absolutely faboo?

*(when **DONNA** doesn't answer)*

Okay I'll tell you. You just take that knife of yours and you do a little trimming. You cut a head off here, you cut a head off there and pretty soon...fabicimo. An arrangement of flowerless stems.

DONNA. It's off.

ROBBY. It is rather off isn't it?

DONNA. I mean we're not doing it. It's off.

ROBBY. What do you mean?

DONNA. I mean I changed my mind. We're not doing it.

ROBBY. What? No.

(**DONNA** *says nothing.*)

Donna, okay, we don't have to cut the heads off the things. We could do it another way, a little less...I could get into a traffic accident on the way. Or get attacked by a band of youth. Or I could just forget the directions to the club. They'd just fire me then. You wouldn't take the blame.

DONNA. *(in wonder)* She asked my advice.

ROBBY. So what?

(**DONNA** *says nothing.*)

Donna...we decided.

(**DONNA** *says nothing.*)

I took the steering wheel from my brother's car!

(a beat)

DONNA. *(to herself, still in awe)* She apologized. She actually apologized.

(a beat)

Robby.

ROBBY. What?

DONNA. I'm sorry.

ROBBY. I thought we were going to do this.

(**DONNA** *says nothing. A beat.*)

ROBBY. Fine.

(**ROBBY** *goes and angrily grabs a crate. He goes to the foot of the stairs.*)

ROBBY. Then I'll bring the crates out to the van.

(**ROBBY** *waits.* **DONNA** *doesn't relent.*)

ROBBY. I'm going up…

> (**DONNA** *says nothing.* **ROBBY** *storms off to the stairs. After a moment he comes back down.*)

DONNA. What's wrong?

ROBBY. The door to the office. It's stuck.

> (**ROBBY** *gets a flashlight.*)

DONNA. What do you mean it's stuck?

ROBBY. I don't know.

> (**ROBBY** *exits to the stairs.*)

ROBBY. *(offstage)* Oh no. Oh no. Shit.

DONNA. What? What is it?

> (**ROBBY** *re-enters.*)

ROBBY. It's not stuck. It's locked.

DONNA. What do you mean?

ROBBY. It – it doesn't open from this side.

> *(dreading to tell her)*

> She locked us in.

> *(a beat)*

DONNA. You told her.

ROBBY. What? No.

DONNA. She knew. She must have known something.

ROBBY. I didn't tell her.

DONNA. Bullshit, you told her when you were working upstairs, when you requested to work upstairs.

ROBBY. I never did that.

DONNA. Then where were you? You weren't down here. Huh? Actions – actions speak louder than words.

ROBBY. I didn't tell her anything. I swear. I swear to God. I have no idea how she knew.

DONNA. *(a tempest building)* It was all a bunch of bullshit. Her apology. All of it. I bet she didn't know. I bet she locked me down here just in case.

(notices **ROBBY***)*

What the hell are you smiling about?

ROBBY. *(exuberant)* The flowers. They're down here. She locked us in, so what. The flowers are down here.

DONNA. It doesn't matter.

ROBBY. Of course it does.

DONNA. *She prepared for this*! "Give me your advice Donna, you handled Gwyneth so well. What do I tell her, Donna, if it doesn't go exactly as planned?" No, she made other arrangements. She did.

It's over. She'll stay in this place, with her *partner* that won't let her have a baby, and pretend that's not what she's wanted her entire fucking life. And she locks me down here. You stupid, stupid bitch. You can't lock me down here.

(looking up to the office)

YOU CANNOT LOCK ME DOWN HERE!

(pause)

(realizing) She cut me off. Like one of her fucking flowers. She cut me off.

ROBBY. Donna…it's not so bad. The two of us down here for the night. It'll be like a date. We'll have fun together. I can see it now. Late tonight, or tomorrow, Ros comes back, finds us giggling together, a lovely evening spent. It'll drive her nuts.

(meaning the work table with the arrangement on it)

Oh, wait a minute. Look. Look over here. I believe it's our table. I believe our table is ready.

DONNA. Robby.

ROBBY. You're right, you're right. I don't like that table either. And I certainly don't like that dreadful arrangement on top of it. I think we can do better.

*(***ROBBY*** exits to the back.)*

DONNA. Robby.

ROBBY *(offstage)* Hold on now.

> *(**ROBBY** returns from the back. He wears a ridiculous period hat with fake flowers in it. In his arms, a large bottle of tequila, two plastic cups, a short faux Greek pedestal, and a second ridiculous hat.)*

ROBBY. There.

> *(He places the pedestal down as a table between their two chairs. He sets the table with the tequila, the two cups and some of **DONNA**'s hamburgers. He hands the second hat to **DONNA**.)*

ROBBY. Better, don't you think?

> *(**DONNA** holds the hat in her hands, says nothing.)*

ROBBY. You don't like the hat.

DONNA. Robby, stop.

ROBBY. Not to worry. There are plenty of others back there. Plenty. I told you, everything in the world, it's all back there.

> *(a beat)*

DONNA. Say that again.

ROBBY. There's everything in the world back there. Like your poem.

> *(picks up the tequila bottle)*

We'll ingest it all! What do you say?

DONNA. I say that's…that's a great idea.

> *(**DONNA** dons her hat.)*

I'm ready.

ROBBY. *(smiles)* Allow me madame.

> *(**ROBBY** pours them each a shot. He raises his cup.)*

ROBBY. Here's to…here's to…

DONNA. Tonight. Here's to tonight.

> *(They touch cups, then throw down their shots.)*

(Lights fade on **ROBBY** *and* **DONNA**...*come up on* **ROS** *and* **KEITH**'s *apartment. Later. A table. Empty.* **KEITH** *sits stiffly at one end. A beat or two before* **ROS** *enters. She's just come from the wedding. She stands at the other side of the table. She holds an elegant bowl filled with fruit. She stands there for a beat, amazed.)*

ROS. They went for it. The Pierponts. I whispered it to them after the ceremony. And they loved the idea. Last minute inspiration is what I told them. Like all great artists. Then I fed them some nonsense about having no flowers that compete with the bride's. It was – outlandish. But they bought it.

*(***KEITH*** says nothing. A beat.)*

So, I was on my way home and I thought – now don't get upset – but I thought since tonight was such a rousing success, we could maybe – celebrate a little.

*(***KEITH*** says nothing. **ROS** places a single Hershey's Kiss on the table.)*

I know, I know. But it's only ceremonial. And, well, we haven't had chocolate in forever.

*(***KEITH*** looks at the kiss on the table then up at **ROS**. He rises. He reaches down to his zipper and slowly undoes it.)*

ROS. *(cont.)* Keith?

(He reaches into his fly and pulls a king-sized snickers bar from inside his pants.)

Oh my God.

*(***KEITH*** goes to **ROS**. He holds the candy up before her.)*

(nearly breathless) Keith.

*(***KEITH*** puts one end of the king-sized Snickers in his mouth, wrapping his lips around it. He leans closer toward **ROS**, the other end of the Snickers before her face. **ROS** stares at it a moment, then takes the other end in her mouth. The stand there, lips wrapped around either end. A tableaux. Lights go down on them...)*

(...come up on **DONNA** *and* **ROBBY**. *Same positions as earlier, but many more burgers eaten, and the tequila bottle emptier. They each hold a shot in hand.)*

ROBBY. What do we toast to now?

DONNA. I don't know.

ROBBY. To candy bars!

DONNA. To candy bars.

ROBBY. No, wait. I know. To Gwyneth Pierpont's wedding!

DONNA. Why not? To Gwyneth's wedding. About as different from mine as I can imagine.

(They touch cups, drink. They chase their shots with bites of candy bar. A beat.)

ROBBY. What was yours like?

(a beat)

Sorry. You don't have to –

DONNA. It's okay. There were some nice things about it.

ROBBY. Yeah? What was your favorite part?

DONNA. *(considers, then...)* The first dance. Without question. Scott and I were out there in front of everyone. And for just a little while I was oblivious to the sea of knit eyebrows, and the looks of disbelief and disgust. "How could such a cute man marry that?" Ros working the crowd, whispering in people's ears, "It's for the health insurance, he's sick, he's gay." But I didn't see that. And I didn't feel that. Not from Scott. Not while we were dancing. He made sure of that. Holding me tight, looking in my eyes.

*(***ROBBY*** stares at* **DONNA**. *He rises, exits to the back. He returns with a boombox. He turns it on and scans the stations. A lot of static.)*

DONNA. Robby –

ROBBY. It doesn't get much reception down here but I thought –

(He's found a station. Not the most appropriate music for the moment. Salsa? **ROBBY** *breaks into dance.* **DONNA** *laughs.)*

ROBBY. Think this is ol' Gwyneth's first song?

DONNA. No.

ROBBY. Ayy!

> (**ROBBY** *takes a big swig of the tequila and ridiculously dances his way back to the boombox. He plays with the dial. Static. Another station comes in.*)

> (*A slow song, perhaps in Spanish as well.* **ROBBY** *moves to* **DONNA**. *He puts out his hand.* **DONNA** *takes it, rises. She moves into him. They slow dance. After a beat or two, they lean together.* **ROBBY** *kisses* **DONNA**. *The kiss lingers a moment until* **DONNA** *pushes him away.*)

ROBBY. What's wrong?

DONNA. You think we're going to be together? You and me? Is that what you think?

ROBBY. I don't know.

DONNA. It's going to be me and you living together in some little studio apartment? Is that what you think?

ROBBY. I don't know. We could go somewhere else.

DONNA. Where?

ROBBY. Anywhere.

DONNA. Where?

ROBBY. I don't know. Anywhere. We could go to Montana, be cowboys together. Ride horses across rivers, rustle cattle, shit like that.

> (**DONNA** *can't help but laugh.* **ROBBY** *goes to her.*)

> (*emphatic*) I'm not too frightened to follow through.

> (*He leans in to kiss* **DONNA** *again. She pushes him away.*)

DONNA. It's too late.

> (*With great effort,* **DONNA** *then drops herself down to one knee. And then the other. She kneels before him. She reaches for his pants. She unbuttons them. She slides them down. And, as the lights fade...she ingests him.*)

*(Lights up on **ROS** and **KEITH**'s apartment. **ROS** enters in a robe. She goes to the table. She collects the Hershey's kiss. She exits again to the bedroom, smiling. Lights fade.)*

*(They come up, later, on the basement. **DONNA** sits on a blanket, staring out, as **ROBBY** lies next to her in fetal position, sleeping. Pause.)*

DONNA. Robby?

*(No answer, he's out. **DONNA** gets herself to her feet. She goes to the work table. She finds an unused piece of oasis. She takes a single flower from the Pierpont arrangement and pulls it out. She sticks it into the oasis. She goes over and sets it next to the sleeping **ROBBY**. She rises, looks upstairs.)*

DONNA. You cannot lock me down here.

(She exits to the back of the basement. Blackout.)

Scene Four

*(Morning. The basement. **ROBBY** sits half-dressed on the blanket. He is completely still. **ROS** comes down the stairs. She sees **ROBBY**, the multitude of McDonald's wrappers, the empty tequila bottle, etc. Pause.)*

ROS. *(feeling guilty)* I couldn't take any chances. This party was too important.

*(**ROBBY** says nothing.)*

From the looks of things it wasn't too bad.

*(**ROBBY** says nothing.)*

Where is she?

*(to **ROBBY** but for **DONNA**'s benefit)*

I'd like to share with her how well things went. Tell her the Donna advice worked like a charm.

*(No answer. **ROS** looks at **ROBBY**, who is unmoved. She takes a few steps toward the back of the basement.)*

Donna? Are you back there?

(**ROS** *turns to* **ROBBY**, *then back again.*)

Donna please, I'd really like to talk to you.

(*to* **ROBBY**, *when she gets no answer*)

What's going on?

(**ROBBY** *is too upset to talk.* **ROS** *hesitates, then exits to the back of the basement. She returns. In shock.*)

Call an ambulance. Call an ambulance.

(*Neither of them move.*)

What...what did she do?

ROBBY. She ate everything in the world.

(**ROS** *just stands there a beat or two before* **ROBBY**'s *words at least partially register. She turns to him.*)

ROS. What? What did you just say?

ROBBY. I told her that's what's back there.

(**ROS** *looks toward the backroom.*)

ROS. Oh my God. Oh my God.

(*She exits running up the stairs.* **ROBBY** *remains.*)

(*A beat or two.* **KEITH** *enters tentatively from upstairs. From the foot of the stairs, he looks around the basement.*)

KEITH. Ros is calling 911.

(*a beat then, sensing it*)

It's too late, isn't it?

(**KEITH** *comes into the basement, for the first time. Pause.*)

Ros and I had sex.

(*a beat*)

It was, uh, whatya call it. Unprotected.

(*The sound of an ambulance siren. Blackout.*)

Scene Five

*(Night. **ROBBY** asleep on a bench. The siren bridges the scenes. **DAVID** enters. He raises his binoculars, searches. He sees **ROBBY** in a heap on the bench, but doesn't recognize him. He starts off then stops. He looks again at the bench. He lowers his binoculars and goes cautiously to the bench. He peers in to get a look at his face. He taps the sleeping person on the bench. **ROBBY** rouses. Sees **DAVID**.)*

DAVID. Oh my God, oh my God. I found you. Where have you been?!

ROBBY. Here.

DAVID. Here? How long have you been here?

ROBBY. I don't know.

DAVID. Robby, Jesus Christ. Jesus Christ. I've been calling you, I've been searching everywhere. You had me sick with worry. Sick. Are you okay? Are you hurt?

*(**ROBBY** says nothing.)*

DAVID. I went to the flower shop. To look for you. They told me. About your friend.

*(**ROBBY** leans into **DAVID**, burying his face in his chest, silently crying. **DAVID** puts him arm around him. Pause.)*

DAVID. I remember when you were first brought home from the hospital. I was terrified. I thought, how are we going to keep this tiny thing alive? I didn't understand it. And Mom and Dad seemed awfully cavalier to me. Second time through it I guess. At night, sometimes they'd leave you in your crib and just let you cry. I couldn't take it. I'd go into your room every time. They'd yell at me for doing that, for checking on you. That made me so mad. You were crying.

(small pause)

ROBBY. Please don't cut me off.

DAVID. Robby –

ROBBY. Please. I'll pay it off I swear. I'll make a list of everything. The windows, the spark plugs, everything. The time you missed from work.

DAVID. Okay.

ROBBY. Okay?

DAVID. Yes. Of course. What did you expect me to say?

(**ROBBY** *looks at* **DAVID** *then leans back under his arm.* **DAVID** *holds him as they sit together, staring out before them.*)

Scene Six

(*McDonald's.* **ROS** *sits nervously at a table. Waiting.* **ROBBY** *enters, bringing a tray with a few burgers on it. He puts it down, sits.* **ROS** *looks down at the burgers. Pause.*)

ROS. Did everything – go okay?

ROBBY. Yeah. Fine.

ROS. Oh. Good.

(*pause*)

ROBBY. Should I...?

ROS. I'm pregnant.

ROBBY. Oh.

ROS. Donna was the first one to tell me where babies came from. She told me all a woman needed to do was eat – as much and as many different things as possible. And then a special brew would form inside her, made from every bit of the world.

(*a beat*)

Keith's not exactly – thrilled about the baby. At least I don't think so. I haven't – seen him.

(*A beat.* **ROS** *looks down at her hamburger, then back up to* **ROBBY**.)

I'm ready. Are you?

*(**ROBBY** nods. They unwrap their hamburgers. **ROBBY** grabs his, rises and jumps downstage into spotlight. He holds the hamburger up for display and celebration.)*

ROBBY. Do you know what's been found in here?
   Do you know?
   Everything.
   Everything in the world.
   You name it.
   Hair, finger nails, skin, sweat, rat feces, human feces.
   Keys, coins, jewelry, a bullet, suntan lotion, toilet tissue.
   It's all in there.
   It's no wonder
   then.
   No wonder at all,
   they didn't hesitate
   when I came in.
   Bring it to the back,
   they said.
   Bring it to the back.
   They didn't even care
   to hear her note.
   Requesting her ashes
   be sprinkled in,
   like a spice, like a seasoning,
   like one of the ingredients.
   It's all in there.
   Everything.
   You just have to make the room.

(He holds the burger in the air, then takes a big bite. Blackout.)

End of Play

OTHER TITLES AVAILABLE FROM SAMUEL FRENCH

MOTHERHOUSE

Victor Lodato

Full Length, Drama / 2m, 2f (Conceived for African-American actors, but casts of other races are possible) / Multiple sets

The play follows an African-American family in a low-income neighborhood whose lives are ultimately ruined by their surroundings. Clive arrives unexpectedly at the house of his mother and his sister. He says that he is fleeing from the police - but perhaps it's another one of his delusions. Unbeknownst to him, he has shown up on a tragic anniversary. Three years prior, his sister's child was killed in a brutal shooting. As fate seems bent on shattering the walls, mother Mae valiantly attempts to keep house.

**Mr. Lodato is a 2002-2003 Guggenheim Fellow,
as well as the recipient of the 2002 L. Arnold Weissberger Award
for** *Motherhouse*